SKATING ON MARS

CAROLINE HUNTOON

FEIWEL AND FRIENDS
NEW YORK

A Feiwel and Friends Book
An imprint of Macmillan Publishing Group, LLC
120 Broadway, New York, NY 10271 • mackids.com

Our books may be purchased in bulk for promotional, educational, or
business use. Please contact your local bookseller or the Macmillan Corporate
and Premium Sales Department at (800) 221-7945 ext. 5442 or by email at
MacmillanSpecialMarkets@macmillan.com.

Library of Congress Cataloging-in-Publication Data

Names: Huntoon, Caroline, author.
Title: Skating on Mars / Caroline Huntoon.
Description: First edition. | New York : Feiwel & Friends, 2023. |
    Audience: Ages 8–12. | Audience: Grades 4–6. | Summary: Still coping
    with the death of their father, twelve-year-old Mars tries to figure out
    their place on and off the rink as they navigate being nonbinary in a
    traditionally gendered sport.
Identifiers: LCCN 2022023529 | ISBN 9781250851871 (hardcover)
Subjects: CYAC: Gender identity—Fiction. | Ice skating—Fiction. |
    Grief—Fiction. | LCGFT: Novels.
Classification: LCC PZ7.1.H86419 Sk 2023 | DDC [Fic]—dc23
LC record available at https://lccn.loc.gov/2022023529

First edition, 2023
Book design by L. Whitt
Feiwel and Friends logo designed by Filomena Tuosto
Printed in the United States of America by Sheridan,
Brainerd, Minnesota

ISBN 978-1-250-85187-1 (hardcover)
1   3   5   7   9   10   8   6   4   2

FOR MY MOM,
STILL LOVE YOU

CHAPTER 1

Time with Katya, my figure skating coach, is in high demand. That's why I'm watching the sun rise out of the window of my sister's Honda Accord as we drive to the rink just outside of Detroit at six in the morning. Time on the ice with a coach is a little easier to line up if you're able to skate during the day. And don't go to your seventh-grade classes. Which I'd be okay with. But Mom isn't there yet.

I mean, don't get me wrong. Mom's super supportive of my skating. Always has been. Even when it got harder to make it to the rink because Dad got sick. When he died at the beginning of the summer, she always found a way—a carpool, a Lyft, *some*thing—to get me to the ice. We've been down a driver for a few months, but she never let a practice slip.

She even got me on the ice on the day of Dad's funeral, after the service and the slow drive following the hearse to the cemetery and the burial. We got in the car when it was all over, and Mom said, "Do you want to skate now?" And I did. I really did. More than anything. Because skating . . . that's the one thing I can always seem to do right. The one thing that clicks into place and just *works*. Even with Dad gone.

Maybe Mom worked harder to get me to practice *because* Dad died. Because skating makes me a little lighter, makes me miss Dad a little less. Or maybe because skating was Dad's and my thing, and so Mom is a little protective of the tradition. Now that my sister, Heather, has her license, it's easier. Though, to be honest, I'd rather Mom drove me more. Heather's great and all, but I can tell that she would rather do just about anything than wake up early to cruise down I-94 and sit on the hard, cold bleachers while her sibling practices salchows and toe loops.

I glance over at Heather as she bites back a yawn.

"Thanks for driving," I say. I thank Heather a lot. Or at least, I try to remember to.

"Yeah." Heather's voice is a little distant. Soft with hints of her yawn still lingering.

"It's a big day." I've been psyching myself up about today for two weeks now.

"Yeah? What's up?"

"Katya's assessing my skills so she can design my next competition program."

"You nervous?"

Am I? I'm not really sure. I know what the answer is supposed to be, so I say, "Yeah, I guess."

Heather scoffs. "Whatever, V. We both know you're excited as hell to show off."

I smile a little. She's right. I'm not antsy because I'm nervous. I'm antsy because I'm amped. Excited. I've been working on a triple toe loop, and I really think today might be the day I do it. The thought of springing into the air, whipping around three times, and actually landing on my blade has me giddy.

"Want some tunes?" Heather asks, another yawn taking over the end of the word *tunes* so it stretches out with extra vowel sounds.

"Yeah. Anything is fine."

Heather tosses me the old iPhone she keeps in the car. "Your pick."

I scroll through and land on David Bowie—Dad's favorite. I almost sink into a sad place as my hand hovers over the song title, but I press play and immediately start to sing along. Maybe I'm trying to push away the thought that I'm listening to Bowie without Dad. Maybe I just need to wake up a little. Heather joins in quickly, and by the time we hit the chorus, the two of us are overexaggerating our words and giggling during the instrumental sections. It's easy to be with Heather like this.

▼▲▼

The carefree feel from the car fades away as soon as I step into the rink. Practice is serious. Katya and her husband, Dmitri, moved to the United States from Russia about a year ago, and I'm really lucky I get to skate with her. Even though she doesn't compete regularly anymore, her body is still in peak condition, slim and muscular. She always wears black—a black leotard, black skating tights, and black leg warmers that cover the tops of her black skates. You don't often see female skaters in black skates, but they suit Katya. Between her monochromatic wardrobe and her face, which is snow white, sharp and angular, she gives off some serious no-nonsense vibes.

My wardrobe is decidedly less intimidating: a maroon "Schrute Farms" T-shirt and some worn leggings with one of the knees blown out that I inherited from Heather. And fuzzy socks.

After warm-up, Katya starts putting me through my paces, asking to see certain spins, jumps, and footwork in quick succession.

This all goes pretty well. It should. I've been working on it long enough. I've put hours and hours into making sure that my body can follow through on the setup. So when I land a jump, it's not just about that moment. That jump is proof that all of the work I've done means something. With each landing, my chest puffs out a little more. Why shouldn't I be proud of what I can do?

Heather was right in the car. I'm good at this, and I like having the chance to show off.

Of course, I'd like it more if I had the ice to myself. Instead, there are eleven other skaters with their coaches running through similar routines. They're all girls. That's the way it always is. Eleven girls and me—a skater who looks like they might be a girl . . . but isn't.

I'm nonbinary—or enby, which comes from shortening *nonbinary* to *NB* and then writing it out. Enby. That's me. Not a girl or a boy—something in the middle. It's not something that people see right away. Most don't even know to look for it. Or what they would be looking for. Because, well, enby doesn't mean one thing. That's kind of the whole point.

I only realized that I'm nonbinary recently. Pretty much right when Dad died. I stumbled on the word *enby* on TikTok and fell down an internet rabbit hole. But seeing that word and trying it out in my mind—it was the first time I felt like something fit. Like the world made a little more sense. And I made a little more sense in it.

Unfortunately, realizing I'm nonbinary also changed how I see the world. Made me see how split things are. Like public bathrooms. Those plastic signs always feel a little hostile now. Stamped with those little block people with legs or a triangle: boy or girl. And look, no one gives me side-eye or shoves me against the tiled wall and tells me to get out . . . I just . . . I kind of do that to myself. I look at the two doors leading into two different bathrooms and think, *Huh, there isn't really space for me.* Not in the way there's space for girls and boys.

And then there's skating. Which is separated into men's and women's divisions. No room for someone who might be both and neither.

Honestly, it feels like there's barely any room for girls. The field's crowded. And competitive. More girls than boys get into figure skating in the first place. Maybe their parents sign them up for skating classes instead of soccer teams; maybe it just has some intrinsic feminine appeal. I look around the rink and take stock of them. These girls who have stuck with skating. Who wake up at five in the morning to drag themselves to the rink for ice time. Who spring into the air, knowing they will absolutely fall again and again until they get it right. Even though people think of skating as delicate, it isn't a dainty sport. It's hard-core. And the girls that stick with it? They're hard-core too. In a lot of ways, I'm like those girls.

But more and more, in ways that seem to matter, I'm not.

One skater with long arms and an ombre overskirt glides past me, her leg raised high and straight in an impressive spiral. My eyes trail after her, watching as she deftly and smoothly navigates across the ice. Her black hair is pulled into a tight bun on top of her head. The way she moves is the way I know Katya would like to see me move. It's as if she's gliding underwater, her limbs moving with an exact kind of grace. I've never skated that way. And I'm not jealous, exactly. My skating just isn't graceful. It's powerful. And I'm sure I can do jumps that other girl can't. But . . . I know I can't skate the way she does. Not all flowy and precise.

I'm still thinking about the spiral girl when I push back my leg to prep for my toe loop. As I rotate in the air, I'm thinking about the way her dainty fingers were positioned in front of her as she skated by me. Without meaning to, I look for her and my eyes snag on her high, black bun.

And suddenly, my blade hits the ice, and I topple awkwardly and land—hard—on my butt.

"You're still under-rotating on that toe loop, Veronica," Katya barks out across the ice. Her voice is quite deep, her accent unmistakable. She doesn't skate over to see if I'm okay. She just says, "You need more power. Bend the knee a little more."

I hate falling. I can feel a blush break out across my cheeks. I hate that too. I push myself up from the ice and cut my eyes over to the spiral girl. She's looking at me too. Probably because I fell. My blush deepens, hot embarrassment and anger blooming on my cheeks.

I shove against the ice, and when I get up on my blades, I spring into the air for a little skip—as if to say, *I'm totally fine! Nothing to see here!* Then I'm off again. Thank goodness for skating. I may be angry. I may think the world is unfair. But here . . . when I skate, it's me and gravity. And my anger is a tool in that fight. I gather speed across the glassy surface, turn my body, bend my leg (a little deeper this time), reach my foot back, and launch into the air.

I keep my arms close to my chest as I spin: one, two, three.

I land perfectly.

My hot cheeks round out as I crack a smile. My first triple!

I can't stop myself from coasting around the rink and pumping my fists in the air. I used to think when people did that at the end of sports movies it was kind of cheesy, but now I know that it's totally genuine. I feel incredible. Unstoppable. Superhuman.

"Again," Katya barks out, bringing me back to earth. Or ice, in this case.

My smile grows, turning into an all-out grin. *Again* is Katya's way of saying, *Good job*. I glance back over at the spiral girl, but she's focused on her own practice now, in the middle of a sit spin. I wish she'd been looking when I pulled off a triple instead of when I pulled off a falling-on-my-butt. I brush off my thighs, and do as Katya says.

Again. Again. Again.

As I run through the jumps, landing each one now, I find myself thinking about Dad.

Sometimes, I like to imagine that Dad taught me to skate.

He didn't, not really. I learned to skate in a small group class. The rink provided skates for the lessons. They were made of blue and red plastic and had big buckles so they could be adjusted quickly.

I remember asking Dad why I had to wear them. Why I couldn't wear white skates like everyone else. Dad laughed and pointed out that some people had black skates and some had tan—not everyone had white. I was four, but I really remember that moment. Maybe it was the first time I ever scowled. Because I knew Dad was dodging the question.

"If you get through these lessons and still want to skate,

we'll get you white ones," he whispered as he clipped the plastic buckles in place.

That was all I could think about through those group lessons from then on. Getting those white skates.

"The bribe" (as it came to be known in our household) isn't the story I tell *myself* about learning to skate though. Instead, I focus on the winters on the pond. People like to complain about how cold it gets in Michigan, but I've always loved how, when the temperatures dip low enough for long enough, the pond in the small woods that border our neighborhood freezes over. Some Saturday morning, usually in January, Dad would get up just before the sun, pack our skates into a canvas bag, and drag me down the sidewalk and through the woods for the first skate of the new year. Sometimes I whined a little at the beginning of the walk—about the cold, or the time—but when we made it to the frozen pond, I was always quivering with excitement.

The first time we did it, I remember thinking it felt so different than the rink. The ice was the color of milk and covered in bumps and dips. Even though I had been coached again and again to bend my knees on the ice, some different instinct kicked in on the pond, and I snatched Dad's hand and forced him to drag me around while I kept my legs rail straight.

Eventually, I learned how to skate on the pond. What parts of my training held and what parts I needed to let go. Sometimes, Dad and I would just skate quietly on the ice, listening to the crisp slide of our blades against the frozen surface. Other times, Dad would chase me around, race me from one end to the other. We did most things as a whole family, but skating on the pond—that was just for me and Dad.

Whenever we'd go out, Dad would only wear his old Michigan sweatshirt and a pair of worn jeans. Even if it was absolutely frigid. "You're going to catch a terrible cold," Mom would say (if she was up early enough to catch us sneaking out for a morning skate).

"I've got to be as aerodynamic as possible to beat V," Dad would always respond. Mom would roll her eyes and wink as she said, "We both know she can skate circles around you."

I'd grin back.

But skating on the pond wasn't about winning.

It was just about being.

With Dad.

On ice.

Dad won't be there this winter. I turn my thoughts to how that secret spot in the woods will feel without him. When will it freeze? Will I even want to wake up and trudge through the woods without Dad egging me on about how he's gonna beat me? Suddenly, I feel the chill of the rink air against my bare arms. I'm never cold when I skate. I try to push the picture of me alone at the pond out of my mind, but it keeps sneaking back into my thoughts.

It's gonna be weird skating without Dad there this winter.

At least I'll be able to land a triple.

CHAPTER 2

When practice ends, I'm winded. I pushed hard, at first because I wanted to show Katya everything I could do, but then I moved to single-mindedly trying to make sure I'll always be able to land that triple. To make my muscles remember the bend in my knee and the angle of my body.

I linger on the ice for just a minute and watch as the other skaters make their way to the doorways along the boards. To be honest, I never really talk to anyone at the rink anymore. No one's really grabbed my attention. Except now, there's the spiral girl. I glance over in her direction as she pulls her long hair out of its tight bun and listens to her coach. I reach for my own leftover fishtails that my best friend, Libby, put in over the weekend, and the bottoms are starting to come loose. I tug at the ties and try to dawdle by shoving my hair into a ponytail. But I don't know how to draw out the ponytail process. Like, some girls flip over and some pull their hair halfway through the elastic and plump it in artistic ways. That's not something I ever took the time to figure out. So

I'm sporting a ponytail in about 2.9 seconds, and the girl's still talking to her coach.

Out of the corner of my eye, I see Heather walking down the bleacher steps toward the door. I skate off the ice and sit on one of the benches by the entrance to start slowly untying my skates. Heather comes up and pulls one of her earbuds out.

"What are you doing? Just put on your skate guards and let's go. I've gotta get to class."

I want to argue. To drag out my skate-removal time—something I'm able to do much better than dragging out my hair-fixing time—to give the spiral girl a chance to catch up. But I also don't want to fight with Heather. And I'm worried that I wouldn't know what to say even if the spiral girl wanted to talk. I sigh, wipe off my skates, and sling on my guards. Maybe I'll see the girl again tomorrow.

When Heather drops me off at school, I reach for my skating bag.

"You can just leave it," Heather says.

"Naw, I'm skating with Libby after school."

Heather rolls her eyes as I hoist the heavy bag over my shoulder and make a beeline for the gym locker room. The so-called *girls'* locker room is a lawless land. No one goes in if they can help it, so it's the one place I feel like I can pee—or change my clothes—in peace. I walk into one of the shower stalls that haven't had running water in over a decade, pull off my leggings, and pull on a pair of loose-fitting jeans. I throw a baggy flannel over my T-shirt and shove my skating bag into the corner of the empty stall so I don't have to lug it around all day. My skates are the most precious thing I own, and the shower stalls in the defunct locker room bathroom of Beachwood Middle School are the safest spot I can think of stashing something precious. No one would look here.

Just as I push against the door to leave the locker room, I take a deep breath.

School is way more complicated than skating.

Not the academic work. That I can do.

But Dad died this summer. This is my first time being here without him around. So instead of thinking of me as Veronica, everyone now thinks of me as the girl with the dead dad.

And here's the thing: I don't really want them to know me as either of those things. As Veronica OR the *girl* with the dead dad.

For my whole life I've never quite fit into labels. The words people used to describe me always just felt . . . off. Especially when it came to gender. *Girl* was the default. And it wasn't right. *Boy*, on the other hand, *that* was never on the table. Not because I didn't understand that trans kids existed, I just knew *I* wasn't a boy. And because everyone seemed to think I was a girl, I figured I'd go along with that for a while.

When I'm skating, I shove those feelings away. It's pretty easy to do. I pour my entire being into height when I jump and speed when I spin. I want to stand out on the ice. To be the best. But at school, where girls are wearing their first bras and trying out makeup, and boys are walking with some extra bravado in their step and talking about how they shave even though they probably don't, it's hard to forget that I'm walking through life a little differently. So, at school, I just wish I were invisible.

"How's it going, Veronica?" I look up, and there's Mrs. Hearse, the school counselor. She has a terrible name. I feel bad about thinking that; but, I mean, a lot of the kids she talks to regularly are people who have had someone close to them die. Like me. I wonder if she ever thinks about changing her name.

I want to stop her and tell her that I want to change *my* name. That she should call me something different. That I'm nonbinary. But I know that's going to set off another round of chats in her office, so instead I just mumble, "I'm fine."

"You're here early. Did your mom have to work?"

"No. I had skating practice."

"Before school?"

"Yeah. I go out to Detroit for early practices."

"That's pretty far," says Mrs. Hearse.

"Not really."

This conversation isn't going anywhere. It's like most conversations with Mrs. Hearse. Not because of anything she does. She means well, I guess. But I just want out of those conversations, because every time someone sees me talking to her, they notice me. They have that flicker of,

Oh yeah, I heard something about you in their eyes. And that something is that I'm a kid with a dead dad. Like I said, I just want to be invisible. Talking to the school counselor isn't being invisible.

"Well, have a good day," she says finally, and I dash away down the hall.

Even though I'm in seventh grade, I make my way to the eighth-grade lockers to find Libby. The one great thing about coming to middle school is that I'm at school with my best friend. At least for one more year.

I was worried for a long time that Libby would be too cool to hang out with me when I finally made it to Beachwood. But for all of sixth grade, whenever I trudged up to her in the halls, she never failed to sling an arm around my shoulder and pull me into whatever conversation she was having. Same with the start of this year. I kind of worry that the habit might break someday, but it never does. Her friends opt to totally ignore my existence.

Today is no exception.

Libby's pale, freckled arm settles across my back as I walk up to her circle of friends.

"—totally inappropriate."

"Yeah, but aren't you curious?"

"About how Cyrus rates my butt? No!" Libby is outspoken in her disgust for the notion. A little bell of recognition goes off in my head. "Ratings Lists"—rankings of attractiveness, of body parts, of, well, anything that isn't personality—are a middle school staple, particularly in eighth grade, according to Libby.

"You're just saying that because you have no butt," says one of the girls—Rasha. Rasha is Indian, with smooth, brown skin and black hair that's colored with purple streaks. Today, she's wearing a pair of shorts and a tie-dye crop top. Clearly, she expects everyone to notice her. And they do. I scowl a little.

"What are you smirking at, flat-chested seventh grader?" asks Rasha.

Everyone's eyes snap to me.

It's a first. And I don't like the attention.

But Dad always said that when it came to fight or flight, I was a fighter eleven out of ten times. Even with bad odds. So instead of shrugging and trying to gracelessly change the subject, I stand a little taller. Libby sucks in some air. She's been around me enough to know that I'm no good at backing down from a threat.

"Just seems too bad that you care so much about what boys think." I stole that line. Mom says it about Heather a lot. Or used to. Heather has moved on from the boy-crazy phase and into an obsessive listening-to-songs-on-vinyl period. "And that list sounds super crappy," I add. "So I'm wondering why you're using something like that to put other people down."

I don't bring up her choice words for me about my lack of boobs. To be honest, I hope I stay flat chested forever. What annoys me is that she *thinks* she's being rude when she calls me out like that. It's a bigger conversation though, about the way Rasha thinks she's hurting me versus how she is *actually* hurting me. And I don't want to get into it. Not with Rasha. Not before first bell on a Monday.

"Libby, you really need to knock off bringing your baby sister into our circle."

"I'm not a baby. I'm her friend. But I can take a hint." I walk away then. On my own terms. As my sneakers hit the linoleum flooring, I run my thumb along the pads of my fingers to keep from balling my hand into a fist and try to stop imagining punching Rasha. She's Libby's friend. Libby probably wouldn't like it. I keep telling myself that as I walk. *It might feel good, but Libby wouldn't like it. So it's not worth it.*

My heart is beating hard. Not like it did after practice. It's unsteady now. Banging against my ribs sporadically and insistently. I wish I could run to some ice.

I don't even notice at first when Libby catches up, falling in step beside me as I make my way to the seventh-grade wing.

"We're still on for skating this afternoon, right?"

I jump when she first speaks, but recover quickly. "Of course," I say. I kind of expect my heartbeat to go back to normal now that Libby has found me, but it doesn't. It still feels weird. Jumpy.

"'Cause you seem kind of mad."

"I skate better when I'm mad." I mean it. Or, at least, I

mean that when I'm mad, I would rather skate than do anything else. Skating gives me somewhere to channel my anger.

"Okay . . ." Libby's word hangs there. "Well, I just want you to notice that I'm following you down the hall at the expense of my social game, so maybe don't be mad at *me*?"

I look over at Libby. Her eyebrows are raised, and she's pursing her lips and puffing out her cheeks. It's this silly face that she's done for as long as I've known her.

"Yeah. I just . . ."

"Yeah. I know. They're . . ." Libby shrugs and smiles. My chest tightens a little as I wait for her to finish the sentence. For her to say sorry or something. Instead, she just says, "See you after school, Mars."

Mars. That's Libby's nickname for me. Even before I knew I was enby, she knew something was up and started experimenting with nicknames. Ver, Vic, Vaughn, Ronnie, Nick—none of them seemed to fit. Then she found out that my parents got my name from one of their favorite TV shows, *Veronica Mars*. It was over from then on. In her opinion, not only was it perfect because it had some connection to my birth name, but it also was the name of the god of war.

I've been Mars ever since.

CHAPTER 3

I may be Mars in my mind . . . and to Libby. But at school, teachers still call out "Veronica" during attendance. I acknowledge that they're talking to me. Or about me. Thinking about asking everyone to call me Mars is a little overwhelming. I imagine having that same conversation over and over again—only to have teachers inevitably forget. It wears me out just thinking about it . . . so I accept when they say "Veronica" and move on. Though, more and more, I bristle when I hear that name.

"Nice to see you, Veronica," Ms. Char says as I make my way into her classroom and sit down for social studies.

I nod and pull out my textbook.

"Oh, no textbooks today. We're going to talk about a new project."

When the starting bell rings, Ms. Char says, "Let's start today by thinking about what you already know. When you think about people who have made a lasting impact on the world, who comes to mind?" A few eager hands shoot up. I cross my arms and settle into my desk.

"Martin Luther King, Jr.!"

"Malala."

"Jane Goodall!"

"Oprah."

"Jesus."

"Obama."

"Jeff Bezos."

"Taylor Swift!"

The list goes on for a while. Ms. Char invites a few students up to the board to write the names. Within a couple of minutes the board is full.

"Okay, now take out your cell phones." We do. "Take a picture of this board. For this assignment, these people are off-limits. Anyone on this list . . . nope." She starts handing out directions. I look down at the sheet—a brainstorming exercise. We're going to be doing a project on change and some person we haven't heard of yet. Someone we haven't thought of at all. Someone who made or is making a lasting impact.

I look up at the top of the page. The word "NAME" is printed in all caps with a line after it. I skip that part and move on to the rest of the worksheet. I start mindlessly filling in the blanks, but I'm still thinking about my name. Mars.

I told Dad about Mars. Just before he died. We knew he wasn't doing well. Lymphoma moves fast. Within a few months of the diagnosis, he seemed mostly gone. He spent those last few days propped up in the bed that we had set up in the first-floor office so he didn't have to negotiate the stairs.

It was a little after two in the morning when I crept down to see him. Snuck down the stairs to keep Mom from waking up. I wanted some alone time. Just me and Dad. In the last days of his life, our house had been overrun by relatives and friends—aunts and uncles who wanted to be helpful and encouraging. They often interpreted Dad's blinks and slight adjustments to be signs of how he was listening to me. I was skeptical. Dad wasn't a quiet person. And he wasn't subtle. In those last days, a part of me worried that even though his body was still technically alive, *he* was gone. That I'd already lost him.

When I crawled on the bed in the office and slipped my hand into Dad's, I was relieved to feel that it was warm. I squeezed his hand, and I swear he squeezed mine back.

"Dad," I whispered. "You don't have to say anything. I know . . . stuff is hard now. But . . . I want you to know that . . . I'm . . ." I remember thinking it was stupid. Stupid that I was taking Dad's dying moments to tell him about me. But I had crept down the steps and climbed into the bed, so I pressed on. "I'm going to start going by Mars. Instead of Veronica." I waited for a minute, hoping that Dad would laugh or smile or nod . . . or squeeze my hand.

He didn't.

"I'm gonna keep skating too. And every jump I land is gonna be for you."

I waited again.

Nothing.

"And . . . I'm gonna be okay."

I really hate that the last thing I said to Dad was a lie.

I keep my flannel on but change back into my leggings for the free skate after school. Libby's mom Martha picks us up and spends most of the car ride asking Libby to catalog her homework for the evening. I sit quietly as Libby rattles off how many algebra problems she's got left and what theme she's going to write about for English. When Martha's done grilling her, Libby rolls her eyes and turns to me.

"Mom's getting territorial about homework time because . . ." Libby stops and bites her lip. I have this sinking feeling she's gonna tell me she has a boyfriend that's taking up more of her time or something. "Because I'm doubling my skate practice." She smiles, broad and big. I smile back. It was a sore spot in our friendship when I amped up *my* practice time and started surpassing her skills-wise.

"That's awesome!" I say.

"Yeah, I've got a double practice tonight. Wanna stick around and watch after free skate, Mars?"

I'm not sure if I do, but it's clear that Libby wants me to want to. So I smile and say sure.

The free skate is fun. Easy in a way that reminds me of when I used to skate as a kid. Most people just scoot around the edges of the rink doing laps, leaving the middle free for people to show off jumps and spins. Libby and I take turns trading tricks. She's definitely getting better. A small competitive part of me sparks, and I start to imagine how Libby might react if I landed a triple right here in the middle of free skate. Our back-and-forth naturally ebbs, though, as the end of the hour approaches and people start leaving the rink. It's then that Libby grabs my hand and starts skating through some pairs moves, placing me as the male partner.

She's never done this with me before, and it's not something I know particularly well, but we fall into an easy rhythm, our skates hitting the ice in tandem. I focus on following her footwork as she leads me through the routine. I try to keep my mind on the moves, but they feel a little different because I'm skating as the traditionally male side of the pair. It feels oddly comfortable. Maybe . . . even right? We're skating backward, my hands on her hips, when she pushes close and says, "And, if you were a dude, this is where you would pick me up and throw me."

Suddenly, I'm cold.

I can feel the chill in the air that keeps the ice beneath me solid.

That sense that things felt right? That's gone. What was a brush of excitement is replaced with an odd embarrassment. Part of me doesn't like that Libby swung all the way to dude. Sure, I'm not a girl, but that doesn't mean I'm a boy. There's a world of other options in between.

I let go of Libby and wind up for a flying camel spin. My

foot kicks out behind me as I whirl around, as if to say, *Don't come close to me, or I will shred you.* The hockey buzzer telling everyone to get off the ice goes off while I'm still spinning. Our turn is done.

Libby skates off to the side of the rink to wait for the Zamboni to clean the ice. I glide to the other side to take off my skates and wipe them down. I think about calling Mom to have her pick me up, but from across the rink, Libby catches my eye and mouths, "Stay," while clutching her hands together in an exaggerated begging motion. It's like she wants nothing more in the world than to have me stick around and hang out with her. Which . . . feels good. It's nice to be wanted.

So I opt to stay.

▼▲▼

Libby wasn't kidding about doubling her skating practice.

She isn't alone with her coach. She's got a skating partner with her. He's tall and lithe, with black hair, tawny skin, and some clearly defined muscles in his arms. I can see them because he's wearing a tank top. Show-off.

It's then that I realize that Libby's routine at the end of the free skate wasn't an ad-lib. It's what she's been working on in those extra practices. She's making the jump to pairs skating.

In a lot of ways, it makes sense. Even though she's really strong, Libby is compact. People used to try to tease her for being short, but she was always proud of it. Now it's turned into an asset.

As I watch the pair of them working, I try to think about what this guy's name might be. Something like Derek. Or Eric. Definitely an "ick" of some kind. I know I'm supposed to be watching Libby—she asked me to come—but my eyes keep going back to Derek/Eric. He must be older than Libby. Some eighth-grade boys have gone through growth spurts, but none of them have bulked up yet. I rub my hands over my own arms, feeling the muscles there and wishing they were a little more defined.

As Libby and Derek/Eric skate, I stretch out my calves, pointing and flexing my toes until some of the tension shifts away from my feet. Then I pull my knee to my chest and hug my leg close. And when that tightness eases, I do the same with my other leg. I'm just finishing my stretching when Libby gives a huge wave. "Come down!" she yells.

I nod, grab my things, and trudge down to the side of the rink.

"This is my best friend . . ." She looks at me with wide eyes, and I give her a small nod. "Mars." I smile and give a little wave. Libby has always been good about taking cues from me on my name. Maybe it's because she has two moms. "And this"—Libby does some kind of flourish with her arms toward Derek/Eric—"is my skating partner, Xander."

Is that short for Xanderick?

"Mars, huh?" Xander asks as he reaches a hand out.

I put my hand in his and give it a squeeze. He squeezes back. A little harder than he needs to. "Yeah." I shrug and drop his hand.

"Xander was just saying that he's working on a triple."

"Oh yeah?" I say. I'm going for aloof, but my blood is starting to sing in my veins. I love competing. And I love winning. And there's a part of me that would really love to do a triple right here, right now. I can tell from the way Libby is looking at Xander that she is totally impressed with him and thinks she's very lucky to get to skate with him.

"I finally got my double axel, so a triple's next up," he explains.

I squint a little. "Yeah. Three comes after two. Great work, Sherlock."

"Mars!" Libby squeals, and punches me in the bicep.

"Ow!"

"Why are you being a jerk to everyone I know?" she hisses under her breath.

"Do you know *I've* got a triple?" I blurt out. Because I do. I landed four of them this morning for Katya.

"You don't!" Xander says.

"I'll show you mine if you show me yours," I taunt. My words are bolder than they should be. Sure, I nailed my triple toe loop this morning, but that was the first time. It doesn't matter though. My bag clunks on the ground, and I fish out my skates. I lace them up quickly and step out on the ice.

"Miss!" one of the attendants calls out. I shudder a little. I don't like being called "miss." Not just because it misgenders me. I don't like it because it makes me seem like less. Like I'm the junior version of something.

"It's cool," Xander shouts back. "I just wanna see something."

I'm not really listening to his explanation. I'm already a million miles away, skating over the practice-worn ice and thinking through how it felt to land my toe loop this morning.

"Ladies first," he calls out. I growl. There's something feral in the back of my throat.

I turn around and reach my foot back, but something is off. Before I can stop myself, I'm in the air. But I'm at a weird angle. Almost parallel to the ice. And all I can do is watch as it rises to meet me. Face-first.

Crunch.

My head—just over my eye—starts to throb. I'm flat on the ice. A part of me just wants to wallow for a minute, but I'm not giving Xander the Wonder Boy the satisfaction.

As soon as I'm up and skating again, Xander takes his own lap around the rink to line up for a jump. He lands a clean double axel, safely beating me.

I look over to Libby. She doesn't cheer for Xander like I expect her to. She just gives me a worried look.

Maybe she should call me Hulk instead of Mars. We both know that I turn into someone else when I'm angry.

I take a deep breath, rip off my flannel, and push off again, lining up my own jump path across the diagonal of the ice.

I fell on my butt this morning and landed the next jump. That's just what I'll have to do now. I bend my knee, a little deeper, remembering Katya's advice, and launch myself into the air.

I do it this time. Land the triple. And prove my point.

This is the kind of moment where I'd expect a crowd to start cheering, but my audience is eerily silent.

I skate over to Xander, who has picked up my flannel shirt, and I pull it from him. "I'm not a lady. So, think I'll have the last word."

Xander's eyes narrow slightly, but then he shrugs and skates off. It isn't until he's left the ice that Libby comes up and gives me a hug. I let myself smile then, but it tugs against the spot on my face where I fell before I successfully landed the triple. I smile harder, in spite of the pain.

Worth it.

The skin around my eyebrow has started to bruise by the time I get home.

"Should I see the other guy?" Mom asks.

"Har, har," I mutter as Mom hands me some frozen peas wrapped in a dish towel. They're the same ones Dad used to hand me after an injury. They made the transfer when we moved from our old house a few years before Dad died. It's weird. I've come to think of life in two eras. With Dad and Without Dad. "You don't seem too shocked."

"Martha called. Said you landed a triple toe loop. I'm surprised you didn't tell me."

"I haven't seen you!" My voice comes out a little whiny, and Mom's forehead wrinkles. My stomach drops. I'm not quite able to tell what Mom is feeling, but it doesn't seem good. "It's not a big deal," I say, trying to soothe her. "I've got plenty more triples in me."

Mom takes a deep breath through her nose and pastes on a smile. "Just sad to miss it. We're doing breakfast for dinner. Eggs or toast?"

"Both, please."

"Hungry gi—child." Mom fumbles over the word *girl*. Even though I haven't come out to her, haven't asked her to call me "they" instead of "she," Mom knows something is up. Maybe she's sensed it for a while, known longer than me. I'm not sure. Now I notice how she tries to shift some of her language on her own. I appreciate it, even if I'm not ready to tell her everything yet.

"Athletes have crazy diets," I explain with a laugh.

"Yes, even twelve-year-old athletes."

The eggs are sizzling in the skillet when Heather walks downstairs.

"Oh, hey there, sleepyhead!" Mom sings out a little.

"Teens are supposed to get twelve hours of sleep . . . which is impossible when I have to wake up at five thirty for chauffeur duty," Heather says by way of explanation, and plops down in her seat.

"Heather, remember, we talked about it, and we agreed that—"

"Chill, Mom. I'm not looking for a fight. Just stating a fact. Breakfast for dinner? Do we have Frosted Mini Wheats?"

"If you're tired, you should probably get some proper food in your belly," Mom says.

"Whatever." Heather rolls her eyes as she opens the cabinet, pulls out the orange Mini Wheats box, and clomps back up the stairs. When she comes back down, she's wearing a tight-fitting jumpsuit and some platform sandals. "I'm meeting up with some friends to study," she huffs as she puts the cereal box down and snags the keys from the shell that sits on the edge of our kitchen counter.

Mom plops my eggs and toast in front of me with a clatter.

"Sorry," I say. Because I don't know what else there is to do.

"No. I'm sorry. We'll give Heather a break, and I'll drive you to practice with Katya tomorrow."

I smile a little, looking forward to some time with Mom.

"I can't wait to see that triple."

CHAPTER 4

When I wake up the next morning, the bruise by my eye has mostly faded.

The car ride with Mom feels particularly long because she's chatty. Usually, Mom can take a hint, but not today.

"Maybe on the way you can tell me a little more about this fight you got into . . . ," Mom prompts.

"No fight. I fell," I say, sleep still coating my voice.

Mom pauses for a moment, but then persists. "And school? How's that going?"

"Fine."

"Any big assignments coming up?"

I think about saying no, but quickly decide that school assignments are a relatively safe topic that will take up a fair amount of time. "Uh . . . I've got a project we're working on in social studies. About moments of change."

"Like . . . ?"

"Ms. Char wants us to learn about people who we don't already know. Like, not just Martin Luther King and Rosa

Parks. She wants us to do a project on someone we've never heard of that made a lasting impact on society."

"Any ideas who you might pick?"

"Well, that's the trick. The point is to find someone you didn't already know. So . . ."

"Ah . . . so you don't really know what you are looking for yet."

"Exactly."

We spend the rest of the car ride talking about the project. Mom offers some suggestions, all of whom I've heard of before. I'm relieved that we've managed to dodge talking about Xander.

When I step on the ice, I glance around looking for the spiral girl, but come up empty. I don't see Katya either. Instead, I get flagged down by a tall man in a fitted navy long-sleeve shirt.

"Veronica!" he calls out. "Hello, I'm Dmitri. Katya is my wife. She can't make it today, so you get me."

"Could you call me Mars?" I ask. I'm not sure why I say it. Maybe it's that if this guy is just meeting me for the first time, I want him to know the version of me I am now. Not the one who started skating with Katya months ago.

"Mars?" The *R* kind of gets stuck in his throat. I almost chicken out. Say he can call me V or something, but he doesn't pause long enough for me to cut in and give him an out. It's the first time I'm actually introducing myself as Mars, and I can't figure out if it feels good or terrifying. "Okay. Mars."

He says the name a couple of times, getting the sound in his mouth. "We are starting on your program, yes?"

"Uh, I thought Katya was going to choreograph it?" Part of the point of working with a great coach is being given a great program by someone who knows your strengths and weaknesses. In our last session, Katya saw everything I could do. Dmitri didn't. Besides, I don't know Dmitri. So I'm a little nervous about him swooping in and taking over at this point in the process.

"She talked to me about it. This program should come from you."

I blink. From me? No. Skating has always been about hitting the next challenge. Learning the next skill. About being told what the next move is and working until I can execute. While I understand that some people think of skating as artistic, that's never been my view. I'm technical. There's a right way to do things—and how I feel has very little to do with that.

I'm silent for a long time. Finally, Dmitri offers, "Let's run through your rep." I nod and execute each move he calls out: split jump, triple toe loop, sit spin, mohawk turn, double salchow–double toe loop, counter turn, flying camel spin, step sequence, double flip, layback spin.

I do them all.

"Okay," Dmitri says when I skate back to him. I'm huffing a little but feel good about the moves. "So that's it."

"What?" I ask.

"That's the routine. Those moves in that order."

"Okay . . ." I wait for him to tell me more.

"You can do all of the elements. But now you have to make it yours."

"Okay . . ."

"So, do that."

"How?"

Then he's off, skating through the same choreographic sequence, but there must be some kind of music running through his head, because he angles his neck just so and stretches his arms out in particular ways. He pauses after each move and looks at me, eyebrows raised. I follow, mimicking the steps and his mannerisms. In particular, I pay attention to his hips and hands. I try to will my own hips to stop wiggling and my own hands to hold tension instead of obsessing over finding grace. Even though I've never been very feminine on the ice, trying to skate with Dmitri's masculine flair is hard. It also feels good. Unfamiliar in a way that wakes up some of my muscles.

Dmitri doesn't seem to care about what I'm doing. He just goes on plowing into the skating space of others, and I follow his lead, taking over the ice in a way I never have before.

When we finish the sequence, he lands an elaborate ending pose. I follow his lead again.

My left knee is bent and my right is extended. My right hand is up high in the air, and my left crosses in front of my chest. I'm pretty sure I look like a kid who got cast as a tree in a play because they were super awkward and the director didn't know what else to do with them.

"See, that's not you," Dmitri says.

"What?" I ask.

"It was the same steps, but not what you did before. And not what you should do in your own program."

"Okay . . ." I'm still not really sure what he expects from me.

"You have to find yourself. And the rest will come."

"Yeah," I say, my voice flat and low. In my head, I'm screaming, *JUST TELL ME WHAT TO DO!* And somewhere else altogether, I feel this horrible uncertainty about what Dmitri is telling me to do. Find myself? I'm not lost. That's not the problem. Not really.

But *something* isn't right. And even if Dmitri's words don't ring exactly true, they still make me feel unsettled. Because it isn't just that Dmitri thinks I need to find myself. It's that I need to show myself.

The rest of practice is a blur. Dmitri gives me noncommittal instructions and talks like he doesn't care if I do what he says or not. I have to bite my tongue to keep from badgering him to be more . . . something. He's the one who's supposed to be pushing *me*.

"You don't seem excited. You landed all of the jumps. And your spins looked good," Mom says as we make our way to our van after practice finishes.

I kind of wish Heather had driven me today. She wouldn't

have noticed how down I am, or at least she wouldn't have asked about it. But Mom? She *has* to ask. It's, like, in the Mom Contract or something.

"I'm excited," I say unconvincingly.

"I thought you were working with Katya on this program?"

"She couldn't make it today, so I had Dmitri as a sub," I explain. Though, to be honest, I'm on the same page as Mom. I thought I was supposed to be working with Katya. She's the one who assessed my skills. She's the one who knows me.

"Oh, well, he's very good. Do you think you would rather keep working with him?"

I think about it. I'm not happy at the end of this lesson. I don't feel satisfied in the way I normally do. But I did like skating in a new way with Dmitri, even if he thinks it isn't me.

"Maybe," I hedge. No need to commit to anything.

"When will you bring this routine to competition?"

I shrug.

"Not very talkative today, huh?"

I don't even need to answer *that*.

"Well, how about Starbucks?" Mom finally offers.

"Sure!" I perk up a little.

". . . in exchange for five observations about your life right now."

Ugh. This is a typical Mom move. Swapping Starbucks for secrets.

"No fair," I mumble.

"If I can't bribe you with overpriced morning beverages, then I'm out of ways to communicate. One?"

I cave. "One. I'm a better skater than the boy that Libby is doing pairs with."

Mom knows better than to comment, though I can tell she's dying to ask a follow-up question. "Two?"

"Two. I don't like middle school girls very much. Well, most of them."

"Three?"

"Three. I think I want my next pair of skates to be black. Like Katya's." And Dmitri's.

"Four?"

"Four. I want a vanilla steamer from Starbucks. And a breakfast sandwich."

"Five?"

I take a deep breath. *I don't think I'm a girl.*

I think it. But I don't say it. I'm not ready.

"I miss Dad."

It's a cop-out. I know it is.

We drive in silence to Starbucks.

CHAPTER 5

If there isn't a hockey game, I can usually get on the ice at Four Corners, the local rink, in the evenings. If there's something exciting going on in town that draws people away from practicing, I sometimes even get the rink to myself. I've been skating there ever since I was a kid, so it feels like my home ice.

On Tuesday night, Mom drops me off so she can run and get groceries while I skate. And thanks to some tiny miracle, I'm alone on the ice. This is rare. Special. Something that I need to take advantage of. After I skate a few laps around the rink to scuff up each corner and warm up my legs, I make my way to the small sound booth just off the ice and plug Heather's old iPhone into the speaker system. I scroll to her music and put it on shuffle.

The sound echoes off all the walls, filling the space with tinny music. "Go the Distance" from *Hercules* comes on first. The song is slow and soulful. And a little cheesy. So I skate that way. I run through the list of moves that Dmitri gave me, hitting my jumps when the music crescendos and filling some of the in-between time with graceful flying arms and emphatic fists in the air.

Next up: Queen's "Don't Stop Me Now." The energy on this version of the routine is a little higher, a little looser, and a little wilder. I lean into my edge work more deeply and can hear my skates carving into the ice.

It goes on from there. "Call Me Maybe." "Defying Gravity." "Baby Shark" (why did Heather download that one?). I take on each song. Trying to listen to the music and get the feeling. And trying to see if any of these are going to help me "find myself," as Dmitri put it.

I'm halfway through Rick Astley's "Never Gonna Give You Up" (leave it to Heather to Rickroll me in the middle of practice) when I notice someone in the stands. My heart starts to beat a little harder. The ice is the one place where I like being noticed. But this moment, this time, it feels special and private. Still, I let my natural tendency to be a bit of a show-off on the ice push me to skate a little more aggressively. I'm further propelled by the twinge of anger I feel at someone interrupting me at all. I'm exhausted when the song ends, breathing hard and deep. But I didn't falter during any of the runs. My legs will be jelly in the morning, but they've done their work.

A series of muffled, calculated claps echoes through the building.

"You're good."

I shade my eyes against the lights and look up to see a

tall black-haired boy in a skiing jacket. It's Xander. Libby's skating partner.

"I thought we settled that yesterday," I yell back, cupping my hands to amplify the sound. Why is he here? Can't I just enjoy my ice time in peace?

"When you fell on your face?"

Okay, he's got a point. I skate over to the sound booth to grab the iPhone. My hour's up.

"Skating away from a challenge?"

There it is. That fight-or-flight moment. I jam my toe pick into the ice and pivot around to face Xander.

"Don't see one," I lie. My blood is roaring in my ears. Xander pulls off his coat and squats down to adjust his skate lace. He must have ice time next.

"There's a competition on Sunday in Canton—the Snow Ball. They just run a short program because it's so early. If you can beat me there, I'll concede you're better. For now."

"No one else going to give you a run for your money?"

"Actually, probably no. Believe it or not."

"*I* would," I say with more confidence than I feel. My words sound strange to me.

"So, I'll see you in Canton?"

"Maybe."

I hadn't been planning to compete so soon this year, but Xander's taunt is tantalizing. Maybe it's because Libby has been acting so obsessed with him, and I want to prove that he's not some dude-god. Maybe it's . . . something else.

"We would be in different divisions," I point out. He obviously competes as a boy, and I've always competed as a girl.

"We can compare scores." His answer is simple enough. But there's a part of me that isn't quite satisfied. Judges look for different elements in men's and women's skating. If I skate in a different division, there's a chance that the comparison wouldn't be as accurate as it *could* be. I think back to skating with Libby, when she placed me as the boy, and even though I didn't like it when she called me a dude, the skating itself just felt . . . right. I didn't overthink; I just skated the way I wanted to.

So maybe the best thing to do is . . . compete in the men's division? The thought is a striking one. I stand there for a minute, rolling the idea through my mind. I never thought about competing as a boy before. Sequin skirts and delicate arms have always been a part of skating that I've had to deal with. But what if they weren't? What if I—

"Hello?" Xander's voice interrupts my thoughts. I look at him, still kind of in a daze.

"We'll see," I say. I'm not sure he can hear me, as far away as he is.

Xander shrugs and walks down to step on the ice.

What would it be like to not worry about having delicate arms, and instead lean into the kind of powerful skating I love? Maybe it would be cool to see what it's like to skate like a boy in a competition. To try on a different style.

Or maybe . . . I just want to win.

If I'm going to compete in a few days, I need to figure out the music for my program. And for that, I need my sister. Heather's sitting in her room when we get home. She hasn't really spoken to me since last night's stomp out, but I figure twenty-four hours is long enough to stay away, and it's time to make amends. I knock on her door.

"Go away!" Heather's voice rings out.

"You didn't even ask who was knocking!" I call back sarcastically.

"Don't need to ask, 'cause there are only two people who live here, and Mom knows better."

"Ouch!" I say. Even though Heather's made it clear she wants me to stay out, I give the doorknob a little jiggle. It's not locked, so I turn it and walk in.

Where my room is an homage to all of my skating competitions, Heather's is an homage to all things teen. Her walls are covered in posters for bands, movies, and anime. Under the posters, her walls are painted lilac. Dad helped her paint the walls about two years ago. Even though I think she might want to change the color, I doubt she ever will. I amble over, flop on her bed, and pull her pineapple Squishmallow to my chest.

"I'm sorry you get stuck dragging me around," I say.

"I'm not stuck, and it's not dragging," Heather answers,

her voice lifeless. Her face is lit by the blue light coming from her laptop.

"Well, it doesn't seem like you're too happy about it," I say, picking at the tag on the Squishmallow.

"My happiness has never entered into the equation, V."

There's a part of me that wants to correct her. To ask her to call me Mars. But this isn't really my moment. I replay Heather's words in my head. Her happiness has never entered into the equation. Does she really think that I don't care if she's happy? Does she think Mom doesn't care?

"How are things going for you?" I've had enough conversations with Mom to know how to probe when someone doesn't want to talk. The person who doesn't want to talk is usually me though.

"Well, since you asked, junior year is a disaster."

"How so?"

"Well, it's always a disaster for everyone, so I have no reason to think it wouldn't be a disaster for me too."

"Makes sense." Plus, you know, dead dad. That probably makes for a crummy year, no matter what.

There's a long pause. Heather picks at the skin around her fingernails. I just wait. Without looking at me, she finally says, "I'm thinking about auditioning for the school musical."

"Oh," I say. I'm surprised, but I shouldn't be. Heather has always loved music. It's part of the reason I use her playlists when I'm practicing. "That's cool. What's the show?"

Heather pauses and crinkles her forehead a little bit. "They're doing *Guys and Dolls*."

"Oh," I say. I don't really have much to add to the conversation. I don't know the show, though I kind of hate the idea of someone referring to girls as "dolls." Or . . . more particularly, I really hate the idea of anyone thinking of *me* as a doll.

"When are auditions?" I ask.

"Tomorrow."

Another pause.

I try to give Heather an encouraging nod. It's not really a full-on nod. Maybe it's more of an encouraging subtle head bob.

"I probably don't even have much of a shot, but I figure it might be fun, and . . . well, you go to practice and do all those things. It might be nice to have a performance of my own." She pauses then, and her eyebrows pull together. She looks down at her fingers, which she has picked to bits. We have that habit in common. I look down at my own nerve-worn hands. "Do you think . . . ?"

I look at her. Her eyes are on me now.

"Do you think you'd come, you know, to see the show?"

What a strange question. "Yeah," I say. "Of course, Heather."

Then Heather leans in and hugs me. Really hugs me, like when we were kids. We hugged a lot when we were little. I never got enough of being wrapped in my family's arms. I'm not quite sure when we stopped doing it. Maybe when Dad died? Hugging is more of a With Dad thing. I don't know.

I push away my sad dead dad thoughts and focus on Heather, who seems a little calmer now. More settled. Probably a good time to ask her for my favor.

"I need help with something."

"Oh yeah?" Heather asks. "It's surprising that you'd willingly ask anyone for help."

"Har har, very funny," I say. I fish her old iPhone out of my pocket and hand it over. "I'm trying to find music for my next program. Something that I can skate to."

"I thought your coach usually picked something for you."

I thought so too. "No, Katya's husband, Dmitri, told me I have to find myself or something, so I have to get the music on my own. I tried a bunch of stuff at the rink tonight, but none of it's quite right."

"What are you looking for?"

"I don't know. Something kind of peppy that will keep me energized. Something that amps up the crowd. It's hard to know what to pick, but you know music and you know me. So I thought maybe you could help."

Heather sweeps me up in another hug. "I'd love to!"

"But here's the thing . . . ," I say. My voice is even less sure now. "I need it in, like, two days. And I kinda need the music to not be too frilly."

"You said it has to be *you*. Frills are the furthest thing from my mind."

Just then, my phone rings. A picture of Libby pops up on the display. It's from Halloween last year when she dressed as Dorothy from *The Wizard of Oz*. She invited me to go to a Halloween party with her and her friends—she had big plans that we would all dress up as characters from the same movie. I was assigned the Cowardly Lion, which worked for me because it meant I got to wear a warm and shapeless lion onesie for the evening. Libby's other friends were the Scarecrow, Glinda, and the Wicked Witch of the West. Rasha was supposed to be the Tin Man, but she bailed and dressed up as a cat instead. I spent most of the party trailing after Libby. At the time, I was happy to be included, but looking back, the memory doesn't feel as happy.

"Hi," I say into my phone.

"Mars, did he do it? I can't believe you didn't text me!" Libby's voice is breathless and fast-paced. I almost can't understand her.

"I assume by 'he,' you mean your jerk of a skating partner. And yes. He challenged me to a skating duel or whatever."

Heather gives me a look. I mouth, "Later," and make my way to my own room.

"Oh, this is perfect." Libby draws out the word *perfect* and kind of rolls the *R*.

"What do you know that I don't?"

"Ugh! He would not shut up about that triple of yours being a fluke. And, well, I just exploded. Told him you're a better skater than him any day of the week. That didn't sit so well. And when he wouldn't let it go, I finally told him to let professional judges settle it for him."

I pause. Honestly, I wasn't sure how Libby would feel about me competing against Xander, but the idea that she was the one who orchestrated it had never occurred to me.

"I thought you liked this guy," I say.

"Sure, I do. But I like you more." It feels like a knot in my chest loosens a little when Libby says this. More and more, I've been worried that she's rethinking our friendship and whether I should be a part of her life. The tension with her friends, the challenge from Xander . . . I always worry that Libby will outgrow me. Hearing her say she likes me more than, well, anything else, it's . . . nice.

"And"—Libby's already moving on—"it doesn't do me any good if my skating partner can't objectively assess his competitors. He should be thinking about how to get good enough to compete against you, not that all he has to do is prove that he can."

I've got to hand it to Libby. She may have a funny way of sticking up for me, but she's got my back when it counts.

"Of course, it's not like I can just waltz into this competition. Because . . ." I swallow, because if I am going to do what I think I'm going to do, I'm going to need some help. "I think I want to compete as a boy."

"Ooooh!" Libby sounds . . . excited? "Mars, it's not gonna take that much to get you in the door. It's always just volunteers handling the paperwork. I swear they don't even read

 47

the stuff! And they have day-of registration, so you can just walk in there on Sunday."

"Wow. Okay . . ." She's really thought about this. Spent time on it. Then I start to think about the Snow Ball. When I first thought of competing as a boy, the idea was a tentative one. Something to consider. But Libby's enthusiasm is like a fire, and I quickly realize that I'm dry kindling, quick to catch flame. "I *have* been thinking about cutting my hair," I say, my voice trembling with excitement. "Short."

"Mars, that would be awesome! And you just have to wear slightly baggier pants—just slightly. And some sort of flowy shirt. I mean, why would anyone not assume you're a guy?"

I can hear the smile in her voice, and I can't help but smile too. We're all in now.

"Besides," Libby barrels on. "Aren't you tired of trying to skate like someone you're not? This could be your chance to try on what it's like to be a masc skater."

Masc. It's a word I've read a few times on the internet but never heard someone say in conversation. It's short for *masculine* . . . A lot of times trans folks use it to talk about presenting with a more masculine vibe. Libby says it like it's no big deal. Maybe it's not. Well, maybe it's not a big deal to *her*. But this conversation—it's just not about skating anymore. It's about me. About who I am. I walk over to my bedroom door and shut it to make sure Mom and Heather can't hear.

"Wh-what do you mean?" I press, my voice a little softer.

The phone is quiet then. I can hear a faint hum, but that's it.

Finally, Libby's voice comes over the speaker. "I just . . ." Libby pauses again. Like she doesn't know what to say. Or like she's waiting for me to say it.

So I do.

"I'm nonbinary, Libby. I'm not a boy."

Silence. Again. I kind of expect Libby to shout that she always knew, that she knows me better than I know myself. I mean, I don't really want her to respond that way, but I always thought that Libby kind of knew . . . had sensed and known this part of me. But maybe I was wrong. We're a year apart in age, but maybe the distance is even wider.

"I'm still me though. I'm still Mars."

"Thank you. For telling me." Libby's words are heartfelt, and I can literally feel my muscles unclench. "And *exactly*. Mars, wouldn't it be nice to just go out and *be Mars*?"

"What do you mean?" I ask the question, but I'm already trying on the words. Sure, I'm me. I've been me as long as I've been around. But . . . I've always been a little muffled. And other people have filled those unclear gaps with whatever made *them* comfortable. Even if it didn't make me feel comfortable. What would it be like to be Mars? Not just to me. Not just to Libby. But to everyone.

"I mean, you don't usually skate at this competition," Libby's explaining. "Neither do I. We don't know anyone there, and they don't know us. No one knows anything about you. You can be whoever you want to be that day!"

No one would know anything about me. No one would look at me sadly because they knew my dad died last summer. No one would assume I'm a girl because that's what they've always known me as. I could just be me. And maybe that's what I need.

"So . . . ?" Libby asks.

"Yeah. Okay. I'll beat him."

When Libby hangs up, I open an incognito window on my phone to look up the details of the Snow Ball. Libby's right. There's same-day registration and no prerequisites for competing. The entry fee is low because it's an early season competition with only a short program component. Normal categories—a division for all skaters twelve and under and then men's and women's divisions for older skaters.

Xander will be in the men's division. So that's where I will need to compete.

And that means I can't exactly be enby Mars. I have to be . . . a boy. I start counting the lies I'll have to tell in my head. One—I'm thirteen. Two—I'm a boy. I say them over and over. *I'm thirteen. I'm a boy. I'm thirteen. I'm a boy.*

I keep thinking those words as I get up and walk from my room to the bathroom I share with Heather, so I can look in the mirror. I push back my hair and examine my face. There's nothing inherently feminine or masculine about it. I allow my hands to drift down. Over my flat chest. I almost laugh thinking about how Rasha tried to insult me by calling me flat chested. I've been fearing the inevitable sprouting of breasts that seems to come with middle school ever since I started sixth grade. Fortunately, nothing has shown up on that front, so I don't have to panic just yet. I keep moving my hands down. Over my hips, my small thighs, my strong calves, all the way down to my toes.

I hang there for a minute, let the blood rush to my head. Then I roll my body up and look at myself in the mirror.

Do I really want to do this? Do I want to lie and say I'm a thirteen-year-old boy? I could ignore Xander. Walk away from his challenge and never look in his direction again.

But walking away from a challenge has never been my strong suit.

Besides, as I look at myself in the mirror, I can hardly see any shred of girl-ness. I'm nonbinary, so pushing my appearance a little toward masculine shouldn't be so hard, right?

When I get back to my room, I avoid my homework and scroll through skating costumes for men on my phone. I've never been a huge fan of skating costumes for girls. Sequins and feathers aren't really my style. But if I thought I would get away from that look by competing as a boy, I am sorely mistaken.

Maybe I can just go for black stretchy pants and some kind of mild-mannered shirt. Keep a low profile. I just need to get in, beat Xander, and get out. And really enjoy the look on his face when I win.

CHAPTER 6

W hen I step on the ice in Detroit the next morning, I'm
disappointed to see Dmitri. I'm not used to him yet.
He gives me a wave, says he'll be working with me again
today, and tells me to warm up and run through the program
sequence.

I do. I nail every move. I know the sequence that Dmitri gave me backward and forward. My jumps are high. My
spins are tight.

But when I finish the sequence and skate up to Dmitri, he
only says, "It's okay. Again, please."

At least the guy is polite.

So I do it again.

I nail it again.

"It's okay. Again, please."

We go on like that for almost the full hour. Nail it. Again.
Nail it. Again.

And even though I don't want to—even though I know
I am lucky to get to work with Dmitri at all—I feel myself
getting the tiniest bit annoyed. My mom is paying for the

man's time. Why pay for an hour when we could record him saying, "It's okay. Again, please," and just play that on repeat?

My hour is almost up when I let out an obnoxious noise that is somewhere between a grunt and a moan.

"It's not okay?" Dmitri asks. He's so even. It's like he's made of ice.

"Again?" I say, sarcastically.

"No."

"There's still time left," I point out.

"What will doing it again do?"

I sigh. "I don't know. What did doing it twenty-seven times over and over do?"

"You tell me." Dmitri's voice is flat. It's always flat. He never gives any clues about the answer he's looking for.

"I showed you I could do it."

"That only takes once."

I sigh again, roll my eyes this time. "I showed you I could do it twenty-seven times."

"You only need to do it once for competition."

What's he getting at? No one lands their first and only jump in competition. You work and work and work until you can't work anymore to be able to perform. You drive away doubt and anger until it's just you and the ice and gravity. "Yeah, I only get one chance in competition. I want to make sure that no matter what, I can nail it."

"Ah. Well, seems like you can."

I furrow my brow. What's he getting at?

"Okay, so what now?" I ask. Because I genuinely don't know the answer.

"That's up to you. Do you know how you want to skate?"

I'm not quite sure what he means by "how I want to skate." I mean, I want to skate clean. Perfect. But that's obvious, isn't it? That's what everyone wants.

"Like, my music?" I hedge. "I'm working with my sister on that."

"Your sister? You think she can answer this for you?"

Dmitri leans forward and puts his hand on my shoulder. I don't shrug him off, but I feel myself standing taller. Pushing his hand up toward the rafters with my shoulder.

"Ah. There you are. It is nice to see you."

I'm about to ask what he means, but just then the hockey buzzer goes off. Ice time is over.

I skate toward the boards and off the rink, where my skate guards are waiting for me. I sit on the bench, wipe my blades down, and put on the guards. I move with cool efficiency, hoping the routine will reset me. But it's not working. I'm still . . . mad. Maybe not ready to explode, but I'm definitely not going to be able to let my frustration go. I'm just about to push myself up when a hand lands on my shoulder.

"Sorry!"

I look up, and it's the girl from the other day. The spiral girl. With the bun. And the spiral. And the ombre overskirt. And the incredible smile. *Uh, did I think that?* I look down at my feet.

"I swear, if I'm not on ice, I'm all kinds of awkward," she says as she plops on the bench next to me. I scooch over, but don't get up—even though there's nothing else I really need to do on the bench.

"Do you have that problem?" the girl asks.

"Wired on ice, tired on land?" I clarify. She kind of laughs, and my anger melts a little. I turn to look at her more closely. First, I just look at her hands. Her skin is a few shades darker than mine. Then I dare to take a look at more of her. She looks like what you would imagine when you picture a figure skater. She's probably my age, though she's a little taller; her limbs are long and lean. And even though she claims to be awkward, her fingers are fluid and delicate as she loosens her skates and pulls on a pair of Nike slides.

"Well, are you?" she asks.

"I'm definitely a mess on land." Truer words were never spoken. "The ice is home."

"I know what you mean," says the girl. "I mean, I feel the same way, but when *you* skate it's so clear that you're home. It's . . . you're really great."

I feel my cheeks go hot. Like, in an honest-to-gosh blush. Not an angry blush. The kind that cartoon characters get when someone kisses them. Actually, it's not just my cheeks; it's my neck and my ears too. And probably my back. My knees. I'm confident in my skating abilities, but I'm not used to praise. Especially not from—I cut off the thought. And then I think about how the thought, if I hadn't cut it off, would have been *a cute girl*. And I shut it down again.

I'm just about to get up and bail when she says, "I'm Jade. Maybe we'll run into each other again?"

"Yeah," I say. I go to get up.

"What's your name?"

"Uh . . ." I lick my lips. What's my name again? "Mars."

I reach out my hand, like I'm going to shake or something. But just then Dmitri glides off the ice.

"Mars. Music. Next practice." He says each word like it's its own sentence. I nod quickly, hopeful that I can turn my attention back to Jade before the moment is ruined.

But someone calls her name across the rink, and she bounds off with a wave.

As I pack up my things, I start to think about my assignment.

Music.

I haven't really ever paid much attention to music. Dad was a fan of David Bowie. When he would get home from a stressful day of work or a particularly bad doctor's appointment, he would walk to the living room, turn up the stereo to blast out "Panic in Detroit," and just dance around. He would always say, "I need everyone on the dance floor for this one!" And we would all get lured out to bounce up and down on the floral-patterned rug that Dad's mom gave my parents when they got married. Mom was often the last to join, but eventually she would get up from her perch on the couch and start leaping around the room with the rest of us. At some point in the song, I'd climb up on the couch and jump into Dad's arms, and he'd swing me around and laugh and laugh. The song would finish, and we'd collapse into a heap on the floor, all heaving breaths and tangled in one another's limbs.

A shot of serotonin in four and a half minutes.

I miss that.

I wonder what would happen if I turned on "Panic in Detroit" when I got home. Would Mom and Heather leap up and start dancing? Would they know that something was wrong without me having to explain? And instead of talking about it, would we just dance around and move past it?

But if I do that, Dad's not gonna come bounding out of his office and catch me when I start doing leaps off the couch.

It will just be three of us.

Which probably isn't going to lead to the relief I'm looking for.

And I still won't have music for my routine.

CHAPTER 7

Here's the problem with not being quite a boy or quite a girl. The world just isn't built for me. And without meaning to, people never seem to be able to talk about me in a way that feels right.

Like, if someone bumps into me, they might say, *Sorry, miss.*

Or, if someone is trying to point out who I am from across the room, they might say, *That little dude over there.*

Honestly, the best I can hope for is people looking at me long enough to get confused and question what they were going to say, which means that I get something along the lines of, "Sorry, mi—uh—yo—sorry."

It's kind of a tricky place to be. Wanting to be who I am. But not wanting who I am to instantly make everyone awkward.

I want to be clear: maybe they're uncomfortable. That's fine. It's that there's not a super easy way for them to talk about me. 'Cause, let's be honest. If they're talking *to* me, they just would use *you.*

And *you*? That has no gender. I'm always a you.

But about halfway through social studies on Wednesday, I decide that I'm gonna try to be a "he." At least on Sunday. So I can compete in the Snow Ball. When I finally make up my mind, Ms. Char is putting us in groups for a jigsaw on activism through the ages. I'm glad she's picking the groups and not having us choose our own. She talks through the instructions, about how we will each have different roles in our groups and be responsible for one another's success in the assignment. I pull out my phone and hold it under my desk as I text Libby.

> Me: We're gonna have to do some boy
> practice
> Libby: Yeah!!!!
> Libby: Wanna sleep over 2morrow? I'm
> having people over for my birthday!

It's amazing how quickly Libby texts back during school. Like, do her teachers just not care, or does she have some superhuman power when it comes to messaging under the radar? I start to think through her request. A birthday party? Why am I just hearing about it now? Did she forget to invite me?

I don't have Libby's super texting power, because no sooner do I get a whole mess of emojis from her than Ms. Char is standing over my desk. She's still talking about the roles of each member of the group, but her hand is out, waiting expectantly.

Busted.

I sink low in my seat and plunk my phone in her hand. At least she didn't make a big fuss. But even though she isn't saying anything, my classmates are looking at me with pity. Everyone uses their phone in class, but no one wants to get caught.

I muddle through the group work. There are four of us—me, two boys, and a girl named Beckie who went to the same elementary school as me. Beckie quickly takes charge, and I let her. My eyes keep drifting over to my phone on Ms. Char's desk, and I'm barely paying attention to whether we're done or not when the bell finally rings and everyone gets up to leave.

"You can stay after for your phone, Veronica," Ms. Char says. I cringe a little and take my time putting my books into my backpack.

Out of the corner of my eye, I see Beckie marching up to the teacher. "Ms. Char," she says. "Let's say *someone* in your group wasn't entirely focused . . ." I roll my eyes and try to tune her out. It's obvious that "someone" is me. Ms. Char manages to say something that calms her down relatively quickly, and Beckie leaves.

I get up and mumble, "It was me. I wasn't focused."

"Hmm . . . ," Ms. Char says. "Well, there are two sides—maybe more—to every story."

"No. There's just the one side. I wasn't paying attention."
I glance down at my phone on the desk.

"Veronica, I'm holding your phone hostage."

This incites panic. It's not just hearing a teacher say the name that isn't mine anymore; it's the idea that I'll have to go much longer without my phone.

"Just until you give me your assignment for our project. The one from Monday."

"Oh!" I say, relief flooding through me. I'm sure I have that. I drop my backpack on the floor and look through all of the loose papers. There it is, a little crumpled but still good.

I go to hand it to Ms. Char. She looks at the paper and says, "Can you put your name on it?"

I skipped that part. I freeze. Just a little. Just long enough for her to smile and say, "Or initials or something. Just 'cause if you don't, I'm going to forget. And then we're going to have this conversation again. Except you won't have the paper in your backpack. It will be in my folder. I'll just have no idea it's yours."

I smile then. Ms. Char is pretty quick to step in for her students. Even when they're using their phone to text their best friend during her class. She doesn't blame anyone for anything that isn't their fault. She just seems to get that being in seventh grade kind of sucks.

I grab a pencil from the mug on her desk and turn the paper toward me.

And I'm not quite sure why, but instead of writing *V*

or *Veronica*—scrawling the end like I tend to do—I write *Mars* across the page and hand it back.

"Mars?" Ms. Char asks. But not in an incredulous way. Not in a judgy way. She just asks.

"Yeah. Could you call me that?"

"Of course." She smiles. "Are you okay with me calling you Mars in class?"

I think for a moment. And nod. Libby has called me Mars for years. It's not so strange.

"What about if I have to write to your parent or something? That okay too?"

I pause for a second. I haven't told Mom. I'm still Veronica to her.

"Can you just give me a heads-up if you're planning to do that?"

"Sure, Mars, whatever you need."

A smile tugs at my mouth as Ms. Char reaches for my phone and places it in my palm. I breathe a little easier as I scroll through sixteen new messages from Libby.

"Thanks."

Libby is all too eager to tell me anything she can about Xander and his program, as outlined in her sixteen text messages that have gone unread while I outed myself to Ms. Char.

Order of elements, soundtrack, components that he might

skip if he isn't feeling on—all of it is handed over with giddy precision and oddly appropriate emojis. I didn't know that Libby had the capacity to be so diabolical. I'm just glad she's on my side.

From there, it takes approximately forty-three minutes for Xander's challenge to grow into a full-on rivalry in my brain. I'm talking a Thor-versus-Loki–sized conflict. Sure, I haven't spoken to the guy more than twice, but even just thinking about his stupid face—which I admittedly can't remember that well, so maybe I'm just thinking about his stupid well-groomed black hair—makes me want to really crush him at the Snow Ball.

By the time lunch rolls around, I'm completely distracted by my own planning. Libby's constant flurry of texts, which continued through English, only encouraged my appetite for rivalry, and all I can think about is: *How am I going to get a costume? How am I going to get to Canton? How am I going to register without getting asked a lot of questions (namely, "How old are you?" and "Are you a boy?")?* The list goes on and on.

"You're going to need to sneak in and watch him skate," Libby says when she plops her lunch next to mine.

"Excuse me?"

"Like, full-on secret agent stuff." Libby's nodding her head and giving me an almost sinister smile.

"I'm better than him. I'll beat him," I say. I'm intrigued by Libby's vision for this challenge, by her commitment and investment in the process. But the pragmatic part of me knows that this is really just going to come down to good skating.

"C'mon, Mars!"

Libby spends the rest of the lunch period insisting that the best way for me to beat Xander is through direct observation.

"We're skating at Arctic Freeze at five. Then Xander has a session with his solo coach at six. You don't skate there much anymore." She gasps like she is getting an idea. *"You could even practice dressing like a boy!"* It's kind of a shouted whisper. She's bringing a lot of chaotic energy. I look over to a neighboring table and see Libby's eighth-grade friends looking in our direction—though they have all chosen to sit . . . well, not with us.

I look back at Libby, who is smiling in that pleading way of hers.

"Okay."

"Oh em gee! Call me the instant you get home so we can talk about what you're going to wear!"

I end up in my baggiest jeans, a hoodie, and a baseball hat. Libby and her mom Deb pick me up to go to the Arctic Freeze.

"What should I call you?" Libby asks as we sit crammed in the way back of the minivan.

"Mars?" I say.

"No. Not Mars. It's too obvious. If someone knows you or goes to school with us or . . ."

"Fine, how about Marv."

"No."

"How about you just tell me what name you're going to call me and get this over with?"

"Alex." Libby smiles.

"That's not—"

"It's perfect. You *look* like an Alex right now."

So I guess I'm Alex. For tonight, at least.

When we get to the Arctic Freeze, Libby heads to the benches to lace up her skates, and I make my way to the bleachers and hike up to the top, where I sit hunched over.

As the hour gets going, skaters fly across the ice, warming up, taking small leaps to test their blades, and working the full length of the ice.

Xander and Libby are spending the practice working on a lift. I take the opportunity to look around the seats of the rink, which are mostly empty. There are a couple of skater moms—moms with ear warmers (unnecessary) and Starbucks cups who record their children when they get the signal. There are a few younger siblings who are hiking up and down the bleachers, playing some kind of elaborate rink tag. There's one lone guy. I guess one *other* lone guy. Besides me. He's leaning back, his legs draped over the bleachers in front of him. The picture of manspreading. I tentatively try out the same position. Extending my legs and leaning into the bleachers behind me. It's uncomfortable. And not my style. Even if I were a dude.

Back to nonbinary hunching.

At about 5:50 p.m., I make my way down the bleachers to grab some food at the Snack Shack.

There's only one other person in line, and as I stand behind them, I start to move my shoulders and shift my stance. *Is this more manly? What about this?* I grind my teeth together and try to push some tension into my jaw. Do dudes really do this all the time? When I feel a tap on my shoulder, I let out a very unmanly squeal and turn around.

And there's Jade. The spiral girl. Not in Detroit, but *here.*

I stare at her brown, almost black eyes as she launches into a quick apology.

"Excuse me. I'm so sorry, but my ice time starts in seven minutes, and if I don't get some food, I'll be pretty worthless. Can I—*Mars?*"

I swear I turn twenty shades of red when she says my name. And I'm not sure whether I should say, *Yes, it's me, Mars,* or *No, I'm Alex, you must have me confused with someone else.*

"It's Jade, remember?"

Oh, God, I didn't say anything and now she just thinks I'm rude and don't remember my own name.

"Hi," I say. Making my voice a little lower. "Go ahead."

She moves past me with an uncertain smile, and I almost give in to the urge to slam my hand into my forehead.

"Thanks . . . ," she says, and runs up to order two granola bars and a yogurt.

Even though her items are grab and go, she doesn't go.

I order a slice of pizza, then step to the side to wait for the person behind the counter to heat it up.

"So, you skating tonight?" Jade asks.

"Uh, no. I'm just watching."

"Oh. That's too bad. It's fun to share the ice with you."

"Yeah, well, we always have brutal morning practices . . ."

"Yeah . . . those! I was thinking that maybe—"

"Alex!" Libby comes bounding up, interrupting Jade. I reach up to fiddle with my hat as Jade gives me a confused look. I kind of shrug, and she looks over her shoulder as if someone just called her name. She's gone, maybe off to wolf down her food, when Libby gets up to me and slings her arm around my shoulder.

"I'm starved, Alex," says Libby.

"Can you stop saying that name over and over?" I say out of the side of my mouth as I reach over and snag my slice of pizza.

"You embarrassed to be seen with me, Al?" Libby leans down and bites the end of my pizza. I roll my eyes and tug the slice away.

"It's Alex. And no. And also, get your own dinner."

Libby is unfazed. "I'm going to get a hot dog and Doritos, and then Operation Defeat X is on."

Once Libby has her food, we head back to the stands. I

almost suggest that we separate, so we don't accidentally tip Xander off, but Libby's already charging for the back of the bleachers where the shadows pretty much make it impossible for skaters on the ice to see us. I sigh and follow.

The next hour passes like many hours have passed between Libby and me. We laugh, we pull up memes on our phones, and we do our best to stay focused on the ice. Honestly, it's a good thing Libby is here to remind me that Xander is who I'm supposed to be spying on, because Jade is on the ice, skating in that underwater way of hers, and I just keep staring.

"Who's that?" Libby finally asks. She smooshes her head against mine so she can match my line of sight.

"Who?"

"That girl. She was talking to you at the Snack Shack."

"Uh . . . just a girl from my practices out in Detroit."

Libby sits back and crosses her arms. "She's very good. Fluid. Probably the kind of person who would beat me in singles. Glad I ditched that world. I wish Xander would do the same so we can really focus on being the best partners possible."

I think for a minute and imagine Jade and Libby competing against each other. Libby's right. Jade is fluid and smooth on the ice. It's hard not to be drawn in by her artistic lines. And I imagine she is the kind of skater who really cares about the connection between their movement and music. Libby, on the other hand, is all about pep and attitude. She's a firecracker on the ice. A tiny ball of energy that just needs a drumbeat to snap into action. Their styles would be different for sure. But, like always, winning would be a matter of technical skill. And I guess on that front, Jade probably has an edge because she's been keeping up with singles skating where Libby has let it go in favor of partnering.

"Um, you're pretty quiet," Libby finally says.

"Just thinking."

"Yeah. Well, focus on Xander. He's strong, but his jumps could be higher. His spins are pretty great though . . ."

I pull my focus over to Xander. At least for a little bit.

CHAPTER 8

I know I should be excited, but whenever I think about Libby's sleepover birthday party, I get a sick feeling in my stomach. It's like I'm on the kind of roller coaster where you keep going higher and higher and higher. And it just seems to keep going. Long enough for you to stop and think about how incredibly high you are. And how incredibly flimsy that metal bar in your lap is.

Dad loved roller coasters. He tracked my height, not in inches, but in what rides I was tall enough to go on at Cedar Point. We started doing an annual summer trip for Heather's birthday when she turned eight. Wilderness Run, Matterhorn, Corkscrew, Maverick . . . each summer I was able to ride a new coaster with Dad and Heather (Mom preferred to keep her feet "on solid ground").

I hit fifty-four inches this summer after he died, which means I can finally ride on Raptor. It was a milestone we'd talked about a lot throughout the winter. Maybe to keep from talking about other things.

It wasn't nearly as exciting to hit that milestone without

Dad. We didn't even take Heather's birthday trip this year. Things got in the way. And, honestly, it would've been weird to go with just Mom and Heather.

I'm still wavering on whether I want to go to Libby's birthday party when classes finish on Thursday. I make my way to Libby's locker out of habit. We usually leave school together.

"Hey, Libby, about tonight . . . ," I say.

"It's my birthday. It's Thursday. There's no school on Friday. You're coming."

I've slept over at Libby's loads of times. Her moms, Martha and Deb, are comfortable enough with me that they yell at me when I do something rude or unsafe in their house (which really isn't that often).

The issue isn't Libby, her house, or the night. It's the fact that it's her birthday, and a birthday sleepover party probably includes other people. People like Rasha.

"It's your birthday," I say. "You want to be with all of your friends."

"You're my friend."

"You know what I mean." I look down. She has to know. She has to see the tension between her eighth-grade friends and me. The way they look at me. Not just because I'm in seventh grade. But because I'm so clearly not like them.

"Please, Mars." There's nothing I can really do when Libby gets earnest. She's giddy and bubbly most of the time, with a dash of sarcasm. Earnest, when it comes, is this rare version of Libby that she demands you pay attention to.

"Yeah, okay. I don't have practice tonight, so I can, uh, come over for a bit . . ."

"For the night. 'Cause, like, the whole point is to stay up all night and then get pancakes in the morning," she says.

"Yeah. Okay."

Libby throws her arms around me in a patented Libby hug. It's very nice.

"Okay, now we've still got to figure out the whole costume thing," Libby says when she pulls away. "Any thoughts?"

"Leggings and a T-shirt?" I say hopefully.

"Wrong! Mars, this is figure skating. Glitz is part of the package, whether you're a boy or a girl."

"But I'm nonbinary," I say. It feels nice to say it. Not as a revelation, but as a known fact in this conversation.

"I'm pretty sure even enby skaters need sparkle when they perform." She loops her arm in mine, and we make our way to the front. "Look, maybe we need a third member of the Operation Defeat X team. What about Heather? She's crafty."

I stumble a little as we walk. I haven't come out to Heather yet. And . . . I've never asked her to lie to Mom.

Just then, Heather pulls the Honda Accord up to the curb.

"Speak of the devil . . . ," Libby says. She kind of sings it, and her voice gets higher and higher as she says the words. "Tell her!" she whisper-shouts as she pushes me toward the car.

"Get in, V!" Heather barks. "I have to get somewhere."

I shove my stuff into the back seat and climb into the car.

Heather's already pulling out of the parking lot before I have the chance to click in my seat belt.

"Where are you off to in such a rush?"

"I have a thing," Heather says, barely pausing at a stop sign.

"What's the thing?" I press.

"If I wanted to tell you, I wouldn't have called it *a thing*," Heather points out.

I take a breath. I'm curious now. I want to know what Heather is sneaking off to do. There's also this part of me that is, I dunno, soothed to learn that she does things I don't know about. It makes me feel less bad about having my own secrets. "I'll tell you a secret if you tell me yours," I offer. "And mine's pretty good."

"I don't care about your secret," Heather scoffs.

Okay. That stings a little. But I brush off the hurt and keep going. "You should. It's so big, I'm even nervous to tell you." I try to sound a little tempting, but the truth is . . . I'm telling the truth. I really *am* nervous about what I'm going to tell Heather.

"How about you tell me, and I'll be the judge?" Heather's eyes are glued to the road, and she doesn't sound convinced.

I take a breath.

Okay. This is it. Time to spill.

"I . . ." My throat closes up a little. Maybe I should rethink this. Tell her later. When she isn't distracted by the road or whatever she is running off to do. Maybe I can figure out the costume on my own . . . or . . . something.

Yeah. Me in charge of costume design? Not a great idea.

"I'm competing in a tournament on Sunday. But Mom doesn't know."

Heather scoffs again. "V, don't take this the wrong way, but that's a terrible secret. You're skating on Sunday. You might as well say you're breathing on Sunday. Skating is, like, all you do."

"No. I . . ." Wow, maybe this isn't such a big deal. Maybe I'm just buying into the Libby drama. I push on. "Mom doesn't know because I'm competing out of my age bracket. And as a boy."

Heather looks at me now. "Why?" she finally asks.

"Because . . ." *Someone dared me*, I think. But boy, does that sound silly. I mean, that *is* why I am competing, isn't it? To prove that I'm as good as Xander . . . or better?

Is there something else though? Something beyond the competition that is luring me to the Snow Ball?

"Because . . . I . . . I'm not sure I want to skate as a girl. So . . . I want to see what skating like a boy is like." I say the words slowly, figuring them out as they leave my mouth.

"What do you mean?" Heather asks. "Skate as a girl? Skate as a boy? You don't get to pick that."

I huff out some air. I'm *not* picking it. I am who I am. I am not a boy or a girl. Libby was so easy with all of this. Got it right away. I've lived with Heather my whole life. How is she not getting it?

"I mean that I'm nonbinary, and I don't really know

which division is the one for me . . . so I am gonna try the men's division on Sunday."

Heather doesn't answer.

My heart starts to hammer. Telling Libby I'm nonbinary was so easy compared to this. Maybe I should laugh and say it's a joke. That I'm competing as a boy, but it's more of a Mulan thing and less of a Demi Lovato thing.

Instead, I ask, "Did you hear me?"

At this point, Heather pulls the car over in the parking lot of a dentist's office.

"Yes. I heard you," she says when the car is stopped. "Geez, Veronica, you can't just spring stuff like that on people."

"Sorry," I mumble, and look down at my feet.

"No, that's not what I—" Heather huffs out a breath. "Look, V, you might want to . . ." Her sentence drifts off and her eyes fall out of focus. "Wait, do you even want to be called Veronica anymore?"

I'm honestly having a hard time tracking Heather's train of thought. She doesn't seem surprised anymore, just . . . concerned, maybe? What did she ask?

"Do you still want me to call you Veronica?" Heather says, a little slower.

"Um . . ." I look at my sister. Her eyes are wide as she looks back at me, just waiting. She wants to know what to call me. She asked. It should be easy. But it isn't. Because even if she really wants to know, I don't know what else will change when I ask Heather to call me Mars. To think of me as Mars.

I look down at my stress-worn fingers. And even though she asked—twice—what if she doesn't really want to know?

I keep expecting her to break the silence. To move on. But she doesn't. Heather just waits. For me to be ready.

I take a deep breath and raise my eyes to meet hers. "I think I like it when people call me Mars."

"Okay," Heather says simply. Then she smiles. Heather got Dad's smile. I swear, she looks just like him when she smiles like that. "Well, you were right, *Mars*, that was a pretty good secret."

I let out a sigh. Okay. That wasn't so bad. Heather's already using my name. And . . . seems like she's in a pretty good mood. A better mood than she was in when I got into her car.

"There's more," I say. Because now it's time for the favor part.

"Does Mom know?" she asks, cutting off my lead-up.

"Um. No," I say honestly. "But I'm gonna tell her." I mean it. I have no reason to hide this from Mom. I'm just waiting for the right moment.

"Okay. You let me know when you do . . . and I'll . . . I mean, we'll all be on the same page then," Heather says. She puts the car in drive and pulls out of the parking lot.

"So . . . there's something else . . . ," I say. Trying to lead into my big ask.

"Okay, well, before you tell me that you're Banksy or whatever, I'm just gonna tell you that I have a callback for the musical at school, so I am gonna need to dump you at home and run off to that."

"What's a callback?" I ask.

"It's, like, a second audition," Heather says.

"Because you messed up the first one?"

"No," Heather says indignantly. "Because I was good in the first one, and they're thinking about giving me a part."

"Oh! That's cool," I say. Good for Heather! If this is a good thing, why does she look like she's about to barf?

"Yes, it's *very* cool." Even though she's agreeing with me, Heather says this kind of aggressively and quickly. Her tone doesn't match her words. "What's your other thing?"

"Well," I say, "I'm hoping you'll help me out, because I need a dude costume for Sunday."

"Fine. Yes. Mars, I will help with that. Now get out."

As soon as I'm out of the car, Heather speeds away—my backpack still captive in the back seat. It's amazing that she's able to move back to business as usual when I feel like I've just tilted our world by sharing my name. The planet keeps spinning, no matter who I am.

Mom drives me over to Libby's at seven.

"Doesn't look like the scene of a wild party . . . ," she says, peering over me into the softly lit windows in the Groh-Stearns' ranch home.

"Mom," I say in a kind of annoyed way. I go to unbuckle my seat belt.

"I'm just kidding."

"It's Libby. It's a birthday party. I think it's gonna be pretty tame."

"Whatever you say. Just don't fall asleep first."

I roll my eyes and give her a smile. I grab my sleeping bag and overnight bag from the back seat and trundle up to the front door.

Both of Libby's moms answer.

"Hey, kiddo!" says Deb. She's really good about finding words that don't assume that I am a boy or a girl. She also has this way of making me feel instantly comfortable. She's short and a little bit bulky in a way that makes it seem like she could beat you up or give you a really nice hug, depending on how she felt. She's also got short hair. For a while she had a long tail—like a Padawan braid. I've seen it in pictures. Now her hair is just short and shaved down on the sides.

"Mars! It's so nice to see you," says Martha. She's tall and has a TV mom haircut. Shortish, but clearly styled. She almost always wears a polo shirt under a sweater or sweater-vest.

I love these women. I lean in and give them a joint hug.

They hug me back.

"I'll take your stuff to Libby's room. She's in the kitchen," says Deb.

Libby's room? I thought for sure we would be in the base-
ment. Libby's pretty popular, and her room isn't small, but it
isn't ten-teens-in-sleeping-bags big.

"Am I the first one here?" I say hopefully. I'm not quite
ready to face the hordes of Libby's friends.

Martha sucks in her breath and waves at me to follow her
toward the kitchen.

"I don't know that many others are coming, Mars."

"No. Everyone's busy? Libby must be bummed."

"Something like that."

Libby is there in the kitchen, a mixer in her hand, batter
flying everywhere.

"Mars!" she shrieks. Martha runs and grabs the mixer just
as it's about to go flying from Libby's hand. "You're here!"

"Yeah. Because you insisted. I thought this was a party."

Libby looks away awkwardly.

Okay, that's two sets of shifty eyes. Not a great sign. I'm
just about to say something when Deb walks in.

"So what movie is on the docket for the birthday girl?
Something old? Something new? A full Lord of the Rings
marathon?"

I take a breath and turn to Deb. "I thought this was Libby's
birthday *party*."

Third set of shifty eyes. *Bingo.*

"No one else is coming, are they?"

Three sets of eyes look down.

"Because I'm here."

And then it's three voices bubbling over themselves to say, "Sweetie, no!" And "We're going to have fun anyway." And "They just don't get it."

I kind of just get numb as they rush to comfort me. I'm not really focused on them. I'm just thinking about what those other girls might've said when they found out they were invited to a sleepover with me. And really, what they said is of little consequence, because they aren't here now. So they voted with their feet.

"What reason did they give you for not coming?" I ask. Because I'm hurt, but I'm also mad.

"Oh, they mostly just had sucky excu—"

"Libby!" Deb cuts Libby off and then turns to me. "It's not important. Libby wanted to spend her birthday with you. So that's what we're doing."

"Yeah, if other people don't like it, they can suck an egg," says Libby. Her moms don't comment on Libby's language this time. In fact, they look a little proud.

"But I understand," says Martha, "that hearing this might make you not feel in much of a party mood. Do you want me to call your mom and have her pick you up?"

I think for a minute. I was nervous about the party. Didn't want to come because of Libby's friends. Now they aren't here. Sure, it feels crappy that they bailed, but I'm less upset for my sake and angrier on Libby's behalf. They abandoned her on her birthday. I'm not gonna do the same. "No. That's okay," I say finally.

"Well, is there anything we can do to shake off this moment and get ready for a fun night?" asks Deb.

I look over at her. At her short hair, and it hits me. If other people are going to act weird around me because they think I'm different, then I might as well *be* different.

"Can you cut my hair like yours?" I ask. I'd been planning on cutting it for the Snow Ball anyway. Might as well make it a thing.

Deb's eyes widen a little, but before she can answer, Martha says, "She can't. But *I* can." She gives Deb a playful bump with her hip, and Deb rolls her eyes.

"It's nice having a wife who can cut your hair every week or so . . ."

Every week or so? Is that what it takes to keep short hair short? I'm just about to rethink this idea when Libby wraps her arms around me and says, "Oooh, I can't wait to see you with short hair."

I pull out my ponytail and run my hands through my nondescript brown hair. And I realize that I can't wait to see me with short hair either.

CHAPTER 9

"It looks *sooooo* good." Libby is full-on giddy as she fawns over my new, short hair while we settle in to watch *A League of Their Own.*

I've gotta admit, I like the look of it.

I always just used to shove my long hair into a ponytail or under a beanie. This, though. This hair feels *cool.* I'm many things, but cool has never been one of them.

My hair is short on the sides, buzzed down close to my scalp. I keep running my hands over those bits because the action makes me shiver. In a good way. The hair on top is a little longer. Martha tried to convince me to fluff it up, but I opt to keep it flat and push it to the left side. Even at its longest, my hair isn't long enough to touch my ears, and I keep combing my hands through it, loving how quickly my fingers run out of hair to touch.

The rest of the night is great. We watch movies, eat too much popcorn, and eventually crash in Libby's bed. It doesn't feel weird at all. Just like the hundreds of other sleepovers we've had over the years. Comfortable and easy.

We spend the wee hours of the morning talking about the Snow Ball and how I'm going to crush Xander. Libby's bravado is contagious, and by the time I drift off to sleep, I'm certain there is no way this guy can take me down. The competition is in a few days, and I still have lots of work to do, but the prospect seems fun.

In the morning, when Mom comes to get me, she just says, "I like your hair."

"That's not much of a reaction . . . ," I say, disappointed.

"I got a Groh-Stearn text and picture. I'm more in the know than you think." Mom gives me one of those mother-knows-best looks, and I get a little worried that she knows *way* more than I think. Like that she knows I am going to register for the Snow Ball as a boy and compete on Sunday in an age division above my own.

But she just smiles and heads back out to the car.

"You too tired for practice today?" she asks. "Deb said you didn't sleep much."

"Are you kidding?"

"What was I thinking? Give up ice time? Impossible!"

I laugh a little. The party's good mood continues to trail after me as we drive home.

When we walk into the house, Heather is sitting at the kitchen table staring at her computer, her hands shaking slightly.

"Heather?" Mom looks over at my sister. "What's wrong, honey?"

"Nothing. I don't think. Can you come and read this?"

I walk over. There's an email pulled up. The subject is "GUYS AND DOLLS Cast List." I suck in my breath, ready to scan the list and not find Heather's name at all. Instead, it's the fourth name down, next to the character Sarah Brown.

"It says you're Sarah Brown," I say.

"It does?!" she nearly screams.

I give her a look of confusion. She knows how to read. This is very clearly laid out.

"I'm Sarah!" she says. "I got . . . I got a part! A lead!"

"Oh, honey, that's wonderful. Congratulations!" Mom gives Heather a hug. After the hug, Heather leaps up like she's been electrified and starts dancing around the house in this kind of jumpy way. It reminds me of Dad's "Panic in Detroit" dance, except that this isn't about getting rid of a bad mood; it's about celebrating a good one.

"I can't believe it. I can't believe it." She says those words over and over.

It's strange. I smile at seeing my sister so happy, but the shock and surprise that accompanies her happiness feels foreign to me. Every win at a competition, I know I've earned. I'm not surprised that I do well. It's like Dmitri said in practice—or like he made me say: I practice enough so I am absolutely sure that I can perform. No matter what. And yes, some of my placement relies on how others do, but I am never in doubt of my own ability.

"Mars! Your hair!" Heather finally says, after she calms down enough to stop jumping all over the kitchen.

I kind of jerk when she uses my name. But it sounds . . . right. If Mom notices that Heather calls me Mars instead of V, she doesn't show it.

"Oh yeah," I say, running my hand through my newly shortened hair. The strands quickly escape and move to rest on my forehead.

"It looks awesome!" she crows.

"Is that the reaction you were looking for?" asks Mom.

I smile and nod. It is. It really is.

Landing the lead doesn't keep Heather from pulling together a playlist of potential skating songs for me. When I go to the rink on Friday afternoon, I start running through the songs right away, trying to figure out which one will work. Which one will let me do all of the moves on Dmitri's list.

I've got to hand it to Heather, the playlist slaps. I go through it, one song at a time, plotting out my routine and seeing how the music fits. Some songs tug at the pace of the program in uncomfortable ways. Some slow me down. I finally settle on "High Hopes," by Panic! At The Disco—a song that I remember hearing in the car a lot when I was younger. The vocals, coupled with an insistent drumbeat, energize my skating, and I can almost imagine the audience clapping along. It's a startling picture. I have always been a disconnected skater. When I skate, it's about me, the ice, and the judges. It's not about the audience. But the idea that an audience could hear my music and see my skating and rise to their feet is kind of exciting.

So I skate.

There are a few other people on the ice, working through their own routines and coaching sessions. I have my earbuds in and work through my routine on my own. I figure out where to leap in the air. When to spin. How my footwork can play with the variations in the song.

The hour flies by, and when my ice time runs out, my heart is zipping in my chest with anticipation. The Snow Ball is in two days, and I have my program. I smile as I unlace my skates and pull them from my feet. I stretch a little and heft my bag over my shoulder to walk out to the parking lot. When I don't see Mom's van, I glance down at my phone.

There's a text.

Mom: Late. Sorry.
Me: Fine. Gonna walk to Lib's

I'm too jazzed to stay in one place. And it's light enough that even Mom can't get worried about the half-mile walk to Libby's house. I type a quick text to Libby to let her know I'm coming, but she doesn't write back.

I put in my earbuds and listen to "High Hopes"—my new song!—over and over. My legs are a little tired after a late night and a hard skate, but I keep pace with the song. I'm almost bouncing. Each time the song runs through, I picture the beats where my elements will hit, how I might add a flourish, how the audience will cheer. Maybe I'll add a second triple.

Maybe I'll complicate my spins. Everything seems possible as the program in my head gets more and more elaborate. *My program.*

The sky is almost purple when I make it to the Groh-Stearns'. The lights are on in all of the windows, and I can see shadows dancing around, running from room to room. Maybe Deb and Martha are having a party. I think about not knocking on the door, about walking past their house and asking Mom to pick me up at the coffee shop a few blocks away so I don't interrupt whatever they have going on. But I'm too excited about my program. I need to share my glee with someone.

So I knock.

Deb answers in a bathrobe.

Okay, so it's not Deb's party.

"Mars?!" she says. "I didn't think—"

Her words are cut off by a series of shrieks.

"If you don't text him, I will! And then you know what will happen, Libster!"

"No way! Give me back the phone!"

I look past Deb.

There's Libby.

And Rasha.

And her other friends. The friends who didn't come to the party last night.

They're here. In her house. At another party.

One that I clearly wasn't supposed to find out about.

Rasha is the first one to see me. She stops dead in her

tracks and gives a sneer as she says, "How did *it* find out about this?"

It.

Is *it* . . . me?

I remember how before, when Libby told me about the party, my stomach felt queasy. Like I was going up and up on a roller coaster. Well, now . . . now I realize that I kept going up, because this moment is the drop. The moment when everything falls out from under me. Because I believed her when Libby said that her friends didn't want to come for a party because I would be there.

More important, I believed her when she told me she chose me over them.

And I was foolish.

Because who would pick a gender-confused, skating-obsessed seventh-grade *it* over a legion of popular eighth-grade girls?

Libby stands still in the doorway, her open-mouthed smile sliding off her face.

"I just came to say that my program is ready, and I'm gonna crush your boyfriend." I don't even think the words. They just come out of my mouth. Like I'm possessed. And before anyone can say anything, I turn around and stomp away. Mom's timing is perfect because she pulls up just then, before anyone can follow me or ask if I'm okay.

I'm not okay. And I really don't want to talk about it.

 88

CHAPTER 10

I opt not to say anything to Mom about Libby's betrayal. She knows something's wrong though.

When we get home, I run to my room and strip off my skating clothes so I can pull on some loose-fitting sweatpants and an extra-large shirt that hangs down to my knees. It's from a turkey trot Dad did years ago.

I don't think of myself as a crier. So I kind of hate it when hot tears start to stream down my cheeks.

I swear. I think of all the words I know that are horrible and ugly, and I yell them. I've never really said these words before. Not like this. I've overheard them. Read them. But I've barely even thought them before now. But in this moment, those are the only words I can think. They are the only words that make sense.

It doesn't take long for Mom to come knocking on the door.

"Sweetie, I just . . ."

"Mom, just go away!" I yell. The words are broken, coming out high-pitched and ragged. I hate them. I hate everything about this moment. I hate Libby. I hate her eighth-grade friends.

I hate me.

"Okay, I'll check back in twenty minutes," Mom says.

I don't respond. What's the point? Mom can be stubborn when she wants to be. She'll be back in twenty minutes.

Mom and Dad used to say I was an unusually reasonable child even when I was, like, four. I guess I didn't really think that screaming would get me anywhere. As I grew up, I learned to just hold on to those screams until I was back on the ice and then throw whatever energy I'd been able to store up into jumping and spinning.

I landed my first double when I was absolutely furious. At school that day, someone had accused me of cheating in gym class, and instead of asking for my side of the story, the teacher had just put me to the back of the line. That was probably the first time I felt the sting of injustice. But I knew I couldn't argue with the teacher, and the other kid was already smugly giving out high fives, so I was just left to fester. That night, when I was at skating practice, all I could do was think about how the teacher had just pointed to the back of the line and nodded. It energized me, so I pushed it into aggressive skating. Into height and speed. After I landed that double, anger was potent in a new way. It was fuel, and under the right conditions, I could burn it into something else.

But I don't have ice to run to right now. I only have my room.

My room isn't really a sanctuary. It's more of a museum. Full of clippings from score sheets, programs from ice shows, and dried flowers from bouquets that people gave me after skates. My closet only has old skating costumes in it. All of my normal clothes are more suited to a dresser—where I just have a drawer for tops and a drawer for bottoms, a drawer for underwear and a drawer for sweatshirts. The bottoms drawer rarely gets closed all the way.

The top of my dresser has one thing on it. Dad's old Michigan sweatshirt. The one he used to wear when he skated on the frozen pond with me. I never want to lose it, and I get worried that if I tuck it in a drawer or hang it off the edge of my bed, it'll get forgotten or swept away. So I keep it front and center. Right on the dresser.

When I'm done screaming, I roll off the bed and walk over to the dresser, where I pick up the gray sweatshirt. Sometimes when I push my face into the material, I swear I can still smell Dad. But when I bring the sweatshirt to my nose, I don't smell much of anything. I try again, and when I can't conjure up the memory of Dad's smell, I throw the sweatshirt back on the dresser and leave the room.

Slamming the door behind me, I stalk to the bathroom, where I crank the lever in the shower up to scalding, strip my clothes off, and climb in. I just let the water wash over me, trying to drive this anger from my mind.

As the heat of the shower beats against my skin, I let my tears pool in my eyes and stream down my face. Salt tears mixing with scalding water. I count to one hundred and slam the lever to cold and try not to shy away from the stream of water as it shifts from piping hot to frigid. I run my hands through the short hair I'm still not used to.

I wait until my breathing is even and then climb out of the shower.

It's odd looking at myself in the mirror. My short hair is sticking up at wild angles. It doesn't look familiar. I don't even feel familiar anymore. My normally white face is red. And splotchy. Mars is the red planet. I'm the red person. I kind of snort/laugh. A weird out-of-body experience. Nothing is funny. My body just needs to do something other than cry.

"Veronica?" Mom calls.

I don't answer.

That's not me.

"I ordered pizza. We even got pineapple."

This is a big concession. Mom and Heather both pooh-pooh fruit on pizza, so the fact that, when I walk into the living room, there is a full pizza covered in just pineapple is huge.

"Wanna watch a movie or something? Old episodes of *Veronica Mars*?"

"Yeah, whatever," I say, my tone lifeless. I pull the blanket from the back of the couch. It's one of those ones you make by tying two pieces of fleece together. Back when I had a whole group of people I skated with, we used to make them for each other to bundle up in the bleachers during competitions. Now as things have gotten more competitive, the number of friends has dwindled, but I've still got the blankets.

I slump down on the couch and let Mom serve up a piece of pizza on a plate and hand it to me.

"There's broccoli too," she says. "I steamed it."

"Okay," I say.

We eat through an episode of *Veronica Mars*. There's a mystery of the week. Veronica solves it. And in the stinger, she gets more information about her best friend's killer.

My best friend's killer is my best friend. There. Solved it.

Mom pauses the DVD and twists on the couch to face me. "Deb called," she says.

I wait. I don't want to talk, but I want to know what Libby's moms said. I always thought they were on my side. And yet they had a party. They hosted those girls who wanted nothing to do with me.

"I'm mad at them." Mom says simply. "They know that."

I blink. Mom doesn't get mad that much. She's an absorber and a peacekeeper.

"I can take their perspective. And I think I understand some of where they were coming from. They want their kid to be happy. To have friends in eighth grade. But I just hope my child wouldn't prioritize those relationships at the expense of other people."

I blink. Friends in eighth grade? Is that how Deb described it? That those girls didn't want to spend the night because

I'm younger than them, so they opted to host some kind of eighth-grade-only party?

It's clear that Deb didn't tell Mom that Rasha called me *it*. Or that Libby pretended that she chose me, when, in reality, she opted to just invite me to some sad side party before the real deal.

I huff. I'm still mad. I look at Mom. Her anger is calm. But now that I am looking for it, I can see it all over her face. Her jaw is clenched so that an odd line runs from her cheek to her chin. Her eyes are shifty—roaming from me to Heather and back again. She can't settle. Anger makes her restless. We have that in common. But Mom is able to contain her restless anger, and mine is written all over my body. It's in the way I wrap my arms around my torso and can't seem to stop cracking my neck.

"I think they want Libby to come over tomorrow and apologize." Mom's words break through.

"Now?" I ask. I sound pathetically hopeful. Mom purses her lips, and I know what she's thinking. My heart plummets. The Groh-Stearns didn't offer to have Libby stop her party to apologize. Tonight? That wasn't on the table. She still gets to have her party. With her terrible eighth-grade friends. I hate how much this hurts. "I don't want an empty apology." I whisper the words.

"Okay."

Heather moves over to the couch and snuggles next to me, almost like she knows I need some help holding myself together. Mom pulls up the remote and starts the next episode.

I watch. But after I shove the hurt away, I move on to thinking about how I can't wait to get on the ice.

And how I hope Libby feels like absolute garbage when she watches me crush her cocky skating partner at the Snow Ball on Sunday.

CHAPTER 11

On Saturday morning, I'm anxious when Mom pulls up to the rink in Detroit. Will Dmitri be my coach today? Will Katya? Do I really know which one I want? And, most important, will they like my routine now that it is complete?

I'm wearing a pair of stretchy dance pants, a kind of puffy pirate shirt, and a vest—all of which Heather dug out of her strange closet. I almost questioned if this was really the best she could do. And then I remembered that without Libby, Heather is the only person I've got to help me get ready for and get me to the Snow Ball. Puffy pirate shirt, vest, and dance pants is better than anything that I would come up with, so I kept my mouth shut. The pirate shirt and the vest are on under my sweatshirt, and I have no intention of showing them the light of day. Not today at least. I have everything on though, to make sure that there won't be a wardrobe malfunction on Sunday.

"Mars!" Jade comes running up as I trudge toward the doors. It's one of those fall mornings that might as well be winter. I can see my breath against the dark sky. A huge puff of steamy air pushes out of my lungs when Jade taps me on the shoulder. I look back at her and nod. My eyes stay focused on her massive bun. She has a lot of hair.

"Nice haircut!" she says. "Did you do it or go somewhere?"

"Uh, a fr—" I almost say that a friend did it. Or a friend's mom. I'm not sure what I'm going to say really, because the word *friend* gets stuck in my throat. "I went somewhere," I finally say.

"They did a nice job. Sometimes I think about cutting off my hair. I've watched enough of those transformation Tik-Toks, and it always looks really satisfying. Was it satisfying?"

It was at the time. Now, so much has happened since I chopped off my hair . . . I kind of forget that it's short. "Uh. Yeah," I mumble. "I feel, well, lighter, I guess."

"I can imagine. Well, it looks great!"

"Thanks."

She's really nice. Like, really, really nice.

I don't feel like I've met a lot of really, really nice people lately.

We keep chatting as we enter the rink. About hair. About skating. Jade shoves down her bulky sweatpants and kicks them off. I try not to stare as she reveals her thick skating tights and leotard. Even changing for practice, she moves with grace and efficiency. After she stuffs her sweats in her bag, we synchronously sit down on one of the benches to put on our skates. It's nice. It's still nice. I keep waiting for it to stop being nice.

"Are you signed up for any competitions soon?" Jade asks.

"Um, trying to figure out my schedule," I say noncommittally. "You?" I'm not sure if I hope she says she's competing in the Snow Ball tomorrow or not. I mean, I want to see her again. But I won't really be *me* at the competition.

"I've got one tomorrow. One of those early ones, ya know?"

I nod. But inside I'm freaking out. Because as far as I know there is only one competition tomorrow: the Snow Ball. And that means that Jade and I will both be there. My mind buzzes with questions. Will I see her there? (I want to.) Should I try to hide from her to keep my cover? (I don't want to, but . . .) Would she even recognize me? (Maybe.) Will she see me skate and be impressed, even if she doesn't recognize me? (I hope so.)

Jade's continuing on. A soft smile accompanies her words. "Just to get the ice under my feet. That's what my coach calls the first competition. She says it doesn't really matter how you do. It's just about getting the ice under you."

"Uh . . . yeah. Sure." I mean, I just want to beat a boy who's older than me and get some version of revenge on my former best friend, so it's not about getting the ice under me or whatever. The Snow Ball is all about winning. It's about beating Xander . . . and now it's also about showing Libby that I can win without her. I lean down and start to tug on my laces, pulling them tight enough that red lines start to sprout across the pads of my fingers.

"You don't feel that way, huh?" Jade says with a light laugh.

"Not really, I guess. I like competing though, so . . ."

"I like skating. Competing is how I get to do that. I'm the fourth child and the only girl, so my parents know how to do soccer and baseball and lacrosse. Anything with a game and a winner. One of my brothers skates too, but he is mega-competitive. And then I came along and, well, competition is how I can get them into it. What I really love is skating in shows, ya know? Maybe I'll be able to chill and just do that someday. In the meantime, just gonna keep the ice under my feet."

By now her skates are on. I'm still working on my second skate when I hear the buzz from the rink saying the new hour is starting.

"See you out there," she says as she heads off toward the rink.

▼▲▼

It's Dmitri *and* Katya who meet me on the ice.

"He says you're good," Katya says, her long blond pony-tail draping over her shoulder. I give Dmitri a look, because I never really got the impression that he was amazed by my skating. He nods at me.

"Says you have been working on your short program," Katya continues. "Do you have music?"

"Uh, yeah. I do," I say.

"Okay, let's warm up and see it."

I skate over to the sound booth and hand over a thumb drive with my song. Then I push off and charge around the ice, feeling the bulky fabric of the pirate shirt under my sweatshirt. The vest is snug, but it seems to hold as I start skating around the ice, launching into a few singles and working my way up to some doubles. The pants feel odd against my skin—too silky. Maybe I should wear tights or leggings under them? I finally work my way up to my triple. I launch into the toe loop and land it solidly. Normally, I would search the boards for Katya to get a nod of approval. Instead, my eyes hunt for Jade, who is doing a footwork sequence. She smiles and gives me a tiny thumbs-up before her coach pulls her attention back to her own practice session. I grin and wind up for a flying entry into a camel spin. Were my pants bothering me before? Things feel fine now.

"Now!" Katya barks out. I know she means that it's time to start my routine. I skate to center ice and give the boy in the sound booth a nod. He yawns and presses play. Panic! At The Disco fills the rink.

It's not uncommon for a skater to go through their routine during a group ice session, especially once we get into competition season. Everyone needs to at some point. It's an unspoken rule that you give that person the right of way during those two minutes and fifteen seconds. So when music comes out over the speakers, everyone kind of pauses and does smaller skills, things that are easy to course correct.

I know from talking to other skaters that people are often self-conscious about skating a routine during group ice time. It's never bugged me.

The routine feels good. My movements are aggressive and punchy as opposed to languid and smooth, the way a lot of other skaters move. Jade and I are so different on the ice. As I work through my elements, I still have to think about what's coming next, but it doesn't pull my focus too much. Just keeps me engaged and in the moment. Some of the music hits are off in this run. That's something to work on. I skate through the routine clean though. I get in all of the jumps, spins, and step sequences that Dmitri asked for.

The cut ends, and I hit a final pose. I don't let it rest the way I would in a competition. I just let my arms collapse quickly and skate over to Katya and Dmitri.

Who don't say anything.

I just stand there for a minute. Wanting to ask them if they liked it. If they are proud. But I stay quiet and wait. I don't want to come across as too needy.

"What would you increase?" Katya asks simply.

"What?" That's all she has to say?

"What difficulty would you increase?"

I let out a sigh. Part of what I like about Katya is her no-nonsense attitude. That she keeps pushing me. I always take that to mean that there are new places I can go. That's part of what I love about skating. I'm good. But I'm not done.

"I could make one of the combos a triple combo. I would have to time it out, but I could add a double toe loop at the end of anything."

Dmitri nods.

"And the step sequence?" Katya asks.

"Um . . ."

"Not a strength. The twizzles could be stronger and more complex," Dmitri chimes in.

I am pretty sure I give him some very serious side-eye. I mean, he's not wrong, but that doesn't mean he has to say it that way. I've spent time perfecting my jumps and speeding up my spins. So my twizzles need work. The step sequence is something that people who can't pull off jumps like to focus on to make themselves feel better about their skating.

Just as I think that, Jade skates by, shifting between edges and moving across the ice in a way that almost seems super-human. And I feel bad for thinking what I just thought about people who are good at footwork. Because *Jade* is one of those people.

"Yes, there's more to great skating than just raw power," Dmitri says. "Refinement can be powerful too."

"I'm twelve. I don't do refinement yet." I sound pretty whiny. I've never whined to a skating coach before.

"Well, it's time," Katya says simply. Maybe she's just brushing past my attitude.

"Fine. I'll practice my footwork," I concede.

Katya pushes off from the boards and launches into a

set of twizzles. "Did you see it all?" she asks when she skates back. "Any questions?"

"No. I got it," I say.

But I don't. I fall. I fall a lot. The opening isn't the problem; it's the continued edge shifts that catch my skates off guard. I can't keep up with the moves, and every so often my toe pick snags on the ice, causing me to stumble. As I continue to hit the sequence again and again, I stop toppling over completely, but my hands brush the ice plenty of times.

"An Achilles' heel, perhaps," Dmitri says.

I've heard the expression before. I don't really know what it means, but my cheeks are burning, and the idea of asking sounds like just about the worst possible thing on the planet. I've done enough talking back for today. Time to keep my mouth shut.

"We'll keep working. First competition in two weeks," Katya says.

Yeah. Two weeks. Or tomorrow.

CHAPTER 12

"Who was Achilles?" I ask Mom as I plop into our van. I shove my skates and bag in the back with little care.

Mom raises an eyebrow in a way that says, *Something's off here*, but she doesn't push. Instead, she answers my question. "He's from Greek history. Or mythology. A warrior."

"That's it? Then where does the term Achilles' heel come from?"

"Oh. Well, in the myth, Achilles's mom dipped him in the river Styx as a baby to make him invulnerable, except the water didn't get on his heel because that's where she was holding him. He fought in the Trojan War. He was pretty lethal until he was shot through the heel and died."

"Ouch." I run my hand down the back of my leg to my heel.

"Yeah."

"The Trojan War is the one with Helen, right? Like, she was really pretty or whatever?"

"That's the one. Helen of Troy."

"A war over a pretty girl sounds kind of petty . . . ," I muse.

"Depends on the girl, I guess," Mom says.

I kind of chuckle. Maybe Helen was like Jade. Interesting and nice and fun to be around.

"How was practice?" Mom asks. "Sorry I couldn't see it."

"Don't be sorry. It wasn't my best."

"Yeah? Was Katya back?"

"Oh, I got double-teamed by the Russian duo," I say. There's a long pause. Having two times the attention should be a good thing, but the only thing that felt good at this practice was talking to Jade. "I've got work to do, I guess."

"Well, that's always true."

I grunt a little.

"Sorry. Was I supposed to go into supportive mom mode? You're a great skater, Veronica. And even great skaters need to keep working."

"Yeah," I mutter. I bet *Veronica* is a great skater. Whoever she is. She's not me anymore.

"Did they talk about competitions at all?"

I feel something kind of slither down my back. I hadn't been planning on telling Mom about the Snow Ball, but I wasn't planning on outright lying to her either . . .

"Uh, I dunno. They said maybe in a couple weeks."

"Oh, I thought some things started sooner than that."

"Yeah. Maybe. I dunno." I shift in my seat a little.

"We can do some research."

Heck of a time to take an interest in when competitions happen, Mom!

She starts to put the van in drive when I see Jade walking out of the rink, her long legs covered in gray sweatpants again.

"Wait, Mom. Can you just hold on a sec?"

I don't wait for an answer as I leap out of the van and run up to Jade.

"Jade, hey!" I say. "I was wondering, can I . . ." I freeze. I can't believe I'm about to ask this girl for her number. Not in a romantic way. But even in a friend way. It feels weird.

I chicken out. A little. "Do you have an Instagram?" I finally say.

"Uh, yeah. I'm @Jade$k8s, with the number eight, and the first *S* is a dollar sign." She scrunches her nose a little. "I thought of the username when I was, like, seven, and I just can't ever think of anything else. Don't judge."

"No judgment," I say, holding up my hands and shrugging.

"Okay. And no judging my cringey photos!" she says. I laugh, trying to imagine if Jade could ever look "cringey."

A car a little way down honks its horn, and Jade jumps. "Gotta run," she says. And she dashes toward a silver Prius. I smile and run back to my van.

"Sorry, Mom."

"It's okay," Mom says. I look over, and she's smiling. She doesn't ask anything, but I can tell she wants to.

"That was Jade. We skate together and she's . . ." Cool? Nice? A good skater? I might have a crush on her? "Anyway, I wanted to say hi."

"Okay . . . ," Mom says, in possibly the most annoying voice on the planet. I openly glare at her, and she takes the hint.

"How is the routine coming?" Mom asks as I snap in my seat belt.

"Fine. I mean, I don't know that I've got it all worked out yet."

"What? You, Veronica, don't have everything figured out in less than a week?" I know she means it as a joke, but her saying that name again makes me squirm.

I told Heather I was going to tell Mom about . . . me. Yes, I'm fibbing about my skating competition plans, but maybe I owe Mom at least *some* of the truth. Really, I owe it to myself. I don't want to startle every time she says "Veronica." I just want to . . . be able to exist with her. I look over at Mom. She's been quiet. Just watching me, her extra-large smile from her early jab starting to droop. Like she's waiting for something.

I take a deep breath.

Now is as good a time as any.

"Mom, can you call me Mars?"

"Mars?" Mom's eyes widen. "Sure. I mean, of course."

"I just, I know that you and Dad really love my name, but . . ."

I feel unsure. And kind of silly. My name, Mars, kind of sounds stupid in my ears. Who am I to change my name to a freaking planet? I can feel my heart starting to hammer. It's not the steady, speedy beat that comes with competition. No. This is erratic and choppy. Like my heart is trying to wedge itself in my ribs to keep from leaping out of my chest.

"It's not yours?" Mom's voice is soft. I can't even look at her.

"Yeah." I pull my knees up to my chin, press my cheeks into them. Even through the fabric of my pants, I can feel how hot my cheeks are. From exertion, from Xander's challenge, from fighting with Libby, from working up the courage to talk with Jade, from finally sharing who I am with Mom and not being quite sure how she's going to take it.

Saying I'm not Veronica to Mom feels . . . personal. Like I don't appreciate something that my parents gave me. Especially Dad, who probably didn't even really hear me when I told him my name on that bed in the office before he died. My breath starts to sputter a little, and I press my eyes against my knees even harder to keep any tears from welling up.

And it isn't just about my name. There is so much more that I want Mom to understand. So I breathe again.

"Part of that is because," I press on, "I'm not a girl. But I'm not a boy either." Another deep breath. I want to look at Mom, but don't. I keep my eyes on the windshield. "I'm nonbinary."

My voice comes out wobbly and broken, so I stop talking and close my eyes. Tight. I try to think about something else. Anything else. I settle on the little spiderwebs that form on the backs of my eyelids when I push them hard enough. Are those veins? Synapses? My thoughts taking some kind of physical form?

"Oh, Mars." This strange feeling runs down my back—it's at odds with the tears that are slowly streaming down my face. "I'm so glad you shared that, Mars." There it is. My name again. I take another breath, but my tears don't stop. I feel hot and uncomfortable. "You don't need to feel bad or embarrassed." Mom slows the van and pulls over. When the van stops, she puts her hand on my back and gives it a gentle rub.

The touch surprises me, and I cry harder. Mom just keeps pushing against my back.

"I hate the way who I am makes everything more compli-cated," I whisper.

"It's okay. Your feelings are valid. You are valid."

"Everything feels hard." I take a deep shuddering breath, hating how my lungs don't seem to be working properly. "Like, I was hoping that telling you would make me feel, I dunno, like, more like myself. But I feel almost the same. Is this how it's supposed to be?" That last question is a whisper. I'm not sure who I'm asking. Mom might be a parent, but that doesn't mean she knows everything—especially about this.

"Oh, Mars." Mom leans over and hugs me.

I let the pieces of me fall apart then. I thought coming out would be the glue that put me together. That made me make sense. But instead, I'm just . . . me. The same. And as I let myself fall apart, everything I've been holding in pours out. "Skating with my coach isn't working the way it normally does, I'm mad at Libby for siding with Rasha—who called me *it*—and even though I want to change my name, I feel . . . sad because I miss Dad so much."

I hadn't planned to say all that. Hadn't been planning on bringing up Dad at all. The truth is, over this past week I've thought of him less than normal. Lately, skating has been about beating Xander, not landing my next jump for Dad—even though I promised him I would make every move for him.

I miss Dad. A lot. But that's not why I'm upset. And it's not why I said what I said.

I know that saying I miss Dad is a get-out-of-jail-free card. It's shorthand in our house for, *Yeah, I know I'm being a jerk, but can you just cut me some slack because my dad died?* Mom always cuts me slack. She always cuts Heather slack. Ever since Dad died—and maybe even for a while before that— she's been this well of patience and support.

Mom's hand keeps moving. She doesn't say anything. Maybe she doesn't know what to say. Or maybe she's busy finding some slack to give me.

"Sorry for losing it," I sputter when I can finally get the words out.

"It's okay. It will all be okay. We'll figure it out," she says. She pulls her hand from my back, and I suddenly feel cold.

Then Mom puts the van in drive, and we pull away from the ice rink.

▼▲▼

Confession: I don't have an Instagram.

But chickening out in my conversation with Jade means that I have to make one if I want to talk to her through DMs.

Or I could just stalk her page for a minute.

Which I do as we drive home from practice. Mom's got a David Bowie CD going.

Jade's Instagram is one of those curated pages with a cultivated aesthetic. The most recent pictures are all of her skating or posing in her skates. But as I scroll back through her content, there are more pictures with other people. She makes a lot of peace signs in her photos with friends and is quick to make goofy faces. Where she normally looks serene and smooth on the ice, her photos with her friends feel silly and almost awkward at times.

I pause on a photo of her with a friend pressing her pink lips to Jade's cheek. Jade's eyes are open wide and looking off to the side of the frame in a kind of *Isn't this dreamy* expression. Her hair, which I always picture in her tight skating bun, is hanging long past her shoulders, a black curtain. The caption reads: **I <3 Love**, with all of the emoji hearts in rainbow order.

I don't know why, but something about the picture makes me think that I could tell Jade I'm nonbinary, and she wouldn't question it. Wouldn't ask me to explain more. That maybe she would just accept that as a part of me.

I keep scrolling. Back to the summer when she went to Lake Michigan with her family. There are photos of sunsets and pictures of her mounted on one of her brothers' shoulders in the water. Snapshots of marshmallows roasting in a fire pit, and a photo where she's waving a sparkler so the tail trails in the air.

When I click on a few photos to read the comment threads, I see that she has responded to most of them with a mix of emojis. All of her replies are joy in emoji form. I keep scrolling, and then I find a black-and-white photo of her resting her head on her arms in a deep windowsill. I click to read the caption:

Not many will get past this opening line, but having one of *those* days & I want to take a moment to remember that it's not all joy and skating. Some days are mellow. Some are painful. I'm here if you need me.

It's strange, reading these words from six months ago. Maybe I would've gone my whole life without ever seeing them, but somehow it seems like they're for me.

I quickly download the Instagram app, lie about my age, and make my own account: **@SkatingOn*Mars***. Without thinking too hard, I snap a picture of the display on Mom's dashboard—the one that says we are listening to "Space Oddity." I throw on a filter, one that makes all of the colors a little brighter, and type **It's a Bowie kind of day**. And hit share.

There. Content.

I find **@Jade$k8s** and click follow.

Within a few minutes, I've got my first mutual.

I smile.

▼▲▼

The rest of Saturday sucks less than Friday.

I'm sitting on the couch working on homework when Heather gets home from rehearsal. I don't want to rush her, so I try to stay focused on reading *New Kid*. Sure, I only read the same speech bubble over and over, but at least it's something.

"Hey, Marzipan! How'd the pants feel?" she asks. I'm not sure how she has already managed to come up with a nickname for me, but here we are.

"I think they'll work. It's just one comp."

"Shirt? Vest?"

"We're in business." I give her a thumbs-up.

"Great. I'm gonna add sequins."

"Well . . ."

"What?" Heather asks.

"I don't want to be too flashy," I whine.

"Um, look, you can compete as a boy in figure skating, but nobody gets to skate drab. Get real."

"I just don't want to draw attention."

"Mars, you are going to be skating. People are going to pay attention."

"When I'm off the ice. I don't want attention *off* the ice," I correct.

"At least let me add a tuxedo stripe and some appliqué on the vest."

"Heather, you have rehearsal. You have homework."

"I have time," she insists.

I might be the brave one in the family, but Heather's the stubborn one.

CHAPTER 13

In addition to serving as my costume designer, Heather offers to be my stand-in coach at the Snow Ball. At about 8:30 a.m.—a pretty darn civil hour, she points out—she drives me to Canton and walks up with me to the registration to pay for my entry.

I hand her the completed form and the twenty-five-dollar fee for registration—leftover birthday money.

I've opted to go with Alex Smith as my name. Nothing extraordinary. Nothing connected to my real name.

I'm shaking when Heather approaches the table and hands over the paper. We decide in order to avoid any possible questioning that I'll head off to the bathroom so the person behind the counter won't look at me and immediately put two and two together.

Of course, the bathroom plan is one I didn't really think through fully, because I'm just about to push my way into the women's room when I realize that, for today at least, I'm a boy. I can't stop shaking as I push into the empty men's room. There are a few urinals along the far wall that I try not to look at as I pivot into one of the stalls. I can barely get my bag in with me, and I sit still for a minute, praying that no one comes in. Just let me struggle in peace.

No one comes in. I think about how the girls' bathrooms are always bustling during tournaments—along with the locker rooms. This is just an empty, calm place.

I pull out my phone and start scrolling through things to calm myself down—and check Instagram.

Jade's been writing back regularly over DM. It might be my imagination, but every message seems a little longer than it needs to be, and she offers more and more details. I try to return the favor, be generous when I can. Truth is, without Libby in my life, it's nice to just talk to someone.

When I pull up Instagram, there's a picture of her. She's got bright red lipstick on—I've never seen her in lipstick before—and a purple bow is tied around her high bun. There's a huge smile plastered across her face and a massive Starbucks cup in her hand.

@Jade$k8s: Comp season means early morning STARBIES! I'm AWAKE!!!

I click up to messages—not yet brave enough to just respond to her pictures openly in the comments. **Good luck today**, I type. I'll have to keep an eye out to avoid bumping into her.

I stay in the bathroom longer than necessary, in part

because someone comes in to wash their hands, and I don't want to leave when they can see me. When I finally emerge, I walk over to Heather. She tells me that I'm skating in the second men's flight, which starts at 11:00 a.m., and I'll be skating sixth. I try to stop shaking and start stretching.

One of the weird things about competitions is you really don't spend much time on the ice during a comp day. You get to warm up with your flight. And then you skate your two minutes and fifteen seconds, and then that's it. As you get better, competitions are a little longer—you skate twice instead of once—but even *that* doesn't seem like a lot. I used to beg Mom to book me ice time on the evenings of competitions because I was so antsy from not getting to skate that much.

After relaying my skating order, Heather quickly slips away to take a spot in the stands. We could've passed her off as my coach and kept her by the boards, but I didn't want to risk having her tied to me in the tournament. Better to just pretend I'm here alone.

I find a place to stash my bag, take off some of my layers, and find an empty hallway to stretch and leap around a bit. It's early still, and the younger division skates first. Then the ladies'. Then the men's. I sneak into the stands to see if I can spot Jade—I'm not sure which division she'll be skating in.

There she is. Warming up with the first flight.

Jade's whole costume is shades of purple with dashes of yellow, white, and black.

I'm not sure how I know, but I can tell she's nervous. Her warm-up is tight, and she's under-rotating in the air. She warms up a spin, and that's no problem. But when she comes back to her axel, she falls the second time and makes it a single the third.

My heart feels like it's burrowing into my chest. Jade's lips are pressed tight together, so I can't see her bright red lipstick as she speeds around the ice again, winds up, and throws out her leg for her double axel. She *just* makes it. I silently think, *Don't do any more during warm-up; you might not have any left for when it counts.* She doesn't listen though. Can't hear me. Doesn't even know I'm here. She keeps attacking axels for the rest of the warm-up. She manages to land all of them, but just barely and always throwing a lot of snow up because she's under-rotating and snagging her toe pick to just hold on. When the warning bell chimes, she halts her attack and moves to footwork, effortlessly flowing through a series of twizzles. She's cooling down, walking through something she knows she can do to soothe her rattled legs.

When the buzzer goes off, everyone clears the ice. Except for Jade.

She's first.

She's skating first.

I hold my breath and watch as she skates to center ice.

She gives a nod toward the sound booth and sets herself for the opening of her program.

The stadium feels unbearably loud to me. People are

talking in the stands. Children are shrieking. Parents are handing out bagels and doughnuts, and sipping coffee from their thermoses.

And all I can think is, *Shut up. You're about to see someone special skate.*

But no one seems to care.

So I hunch down and cup my fingers around my eyes to push every ounce of focus toward Jade. Maybe not everyone will be focused on her, but at least one person will be. That's something.

She starts the program.

"Viva La Vida," by Coldplay, comes on over the speakers, filling the rink with orchestral sounds. Jade opens with a step sequence and a solid sit spin. Then she goes into a double toe loop. I know her axel is coming. It's clearly a stretch for her, so it has to come early in her program before she gets too tired.

She starts cranking across the ice on a diagonal and winds up, getting ready to launch for two and a half revolutions.

But she's short.

Her blade catches on the ice, and she tumbles to the ground.

That's when it gets quiet. No one was paying attention before, but now that she's fallen, everyone's eyes are on her.

I have no air. No voice. No nothing.

But Jade's music keeps going, and she gets up with a massive smile—bigger than the one on Instagram—plastered across her face. She immediately launches into her next spin. It's a moving spin, one where her body contorts throughout the spin to create dizzying shapes. When she pulls out of it, there is some light applause. Next up is another jump. A double salchow combination with a double loop . . . She nails it. More applause. And the huge smile on Jade's lips gets replaced with one that's genuine. Like the one I saw in her picture at the lake. Like the smile she gave me after practice the other day.

When the program ends, there's light applause again, but the excitement of someone falling has passed. Everyone goes back to their coffee and bagels. Their own conversations. Their own lives.

I watch as Jade's score shows up on the screen. There's no way she's getting close to the podium. I wince a little, hurt on her behalf, and sneak out of the bleachers and back to my hall.

It's going to be my turn soon enough.

And even though I'm proud of Jade for delivering a solid skate after falling on her double axel, I know I'm not willing to accept anything less than perfect for my own performance.

▼▲▼

I'm not sure when Xander is supposed to skate.

I'm not even sure he's here.

I'm not sure I care.

Okay, that last one is a lie.

But I try to push all thoughts of Xander out of my head, because the only thing I should be focusing on is my program.

I'm using my phone to play my cut of "High Hopes" over and over when a text comes through.

Libby: X had a clean skate.

And another.

Libby: I'm glad you'll beat him clean.

I don't want Libby to be glad. I want her to be sorry. How can the first thing she types in that phone of hers not be, *Sorry for being such a jerky jerk face?* Ugh!

The puffy sleeves on the pirate shirt are a little flappier than I anticipated. Other than that, when it's my turn to take the ice, warm-up is unremarkable. I work up to my triple and notice a few people eyeing me when I land it a second time. It isn't until I go to step off the ice that I notice my white skates.

It's one of the other guys that brings my attention to them—a tall boy with buzzed hair. "Nice skates," he says sarcastically. I want to punch him. I'm pretty sure that would not be viewed positively by the Michigan Figure Skating Association. And it would probably draw some of that "off the ice" attention I've been insisting I want to avoid.

Crap. I look around. Every other competitor has black skates. I didn't want to stand out, and I do. I sit on the bench when a Black boy, not much taller than me, sidles up.

"Doesn't matter what color your skates are," he mutters. "You can land a triple. I wouldn't care if your skates were hot pink."

"Thanks."

"I'm Ty. I don't think we've met before. What's your name?"

I look back at Ty, curious why he's still talking to me. Suspicious that he's interested.

"Alex," I say, finally. Ty shoves out a hand, and we shake. I kind of expect him to squeeze my knuckles together, the painful way Xander did when we first met. But Ty just pumps my hand up and down and lets it go.

"When do you skate? I'm third."

"Sixth." I want to wrap my arms around myself, to hold my body together, but I notice that Ty is stretching. I start to mimic his moves, throwing in some of my own familiar stretches here and there.

"Ah, last! You either love it or hate it. What's your opinion?"

"Don't have one yet." I roll my shoulders, one at a time.

"Still green." Ty starts rolling his shoulders too.

"Yeah. I guess." This definitely feels new. And I *am* nervous. Something I haven't been on the ice for a while. Every one of these competitors seems bigger, more intimidating. I'm used to petite powerhouse girls . . . but straight-up strong dudes? That's new for me. And scary. And I'm not quite sure what people will see when they see *me* on the ice.

Ty is quiet when other skaters are up, respectful and focused. But as soon as each skater hits his final pose, Ty leans over and asks me my thoughts. I don't say much. He gives his own opinion readily.

Soon, he's up. There's a little applause when he takes the ice. His mom, probably. I think about putting my earbuds back in to listen to my own song one more time, but Ty turns back and smiles in my direction before hitting his opening pose, so I decide to watch.

Ty's program is powerful. He reminds me of Dmitri, though slightly less particular in the placement of his limbs. It's hard not to be impressed by his jumps, but what surprises me is the way he looks out into the audience during his step sequences, almost as if he expects them to be paying very close attention.

He's skating to a classical piece of music. It sounds Halloween-like, and his black outfit is accented with white appliqué bones. The audience is eating it up. Maybe because it's October, and Halloween is just around the corner. Or maybe because Ty is so dang watchable.

When he finishes the skate, I clap my hands together. I kind of hope he'll come back and talk to me about the rest of the skaters, but he's off, talking to his coach, analyzing the skate, and unlacing.

Two more skaters to go. Then me.

I put in my earbuds and try to ignore the way my legs are bouncing up and down out of rhythm with my music.

Even though I'm not watching them with the same attentiveness that I reserved for Ty and Jade, I know both of the other boys who skate just before me are good. Not as good as Ty, but still strong. Definitely competitive. Even though I try not to focus on them, I'm starting to feel less sure of myself. Less certain that I will be able to pull off what I think I can.

I look down at my white skates, stark against the black floor. I wonder if everyone else is looking at my skates too. Wondering why I'm not wearing black like everyone else. Thinking I don't belong.

I'll just have to prove that there's room for me here.

CHAPTER 14

I t's finally my turn. I look up at the screen displaying everyone's scores. Ty leads the pack, and Xander currently sits in third. Skating last means that I either confirm the top three or upset them.

I skate out, thinking about how I've planned for this moment. Sure, Libby and I put together the plot to get me into the competition as a boy, but this part? The skating. The winning. That's all me. And there's always one plan when I'm skating: technical perfection.

"Now skating: Alex Smith."

There is no applause. Just some faint chatter.

I take a lap of the ice. Feel it beneath my feet. Note the spots where other skaters have made divots or spun. Finally, I make my way to center ice, jam my toe pick down, and find my starting position. I nod at the person in the sound booth.

There are five seconds of silence. Those five seconds stretch out, and I imagine what it would be like to skate the way Ty does. To flirt with the audience and make them fall in love. Or the way Jade does. To not care what anyone thinks and love the moments on the ice unconditionally. But I only know one way to skate: my way.

My skating is powerful. I'm not worried about being pretty. I'm focused on getting every aspect right. Perfect.

The vocals for my music kick in, and my pulse jumps.

When people ask why I practice so much, I say it's because I can only mess up so many times. There's a finite number, and practice gets them out of my system.

There are some things about competition, however, you can't practice for.

I can't practice the way my heart beats a little faster than normal.

The way I can feel the bottom button of my vest straining against its thread.

The way I swear the light is reflecting off my bright white skates.

Even though I can't practice those things, practice can still help with them. Because if I practice enough, those little things won't make a discernible difference to anyone but me.

Once I get past the triple, I know there's nothing that can stop me from delivering the rest of the program. I'm beaming as I take my next turn.

Practice doesn't give me this feeling either.

Absolute euphoria.

Dmitri might like to say that my footwork is my Achilles'

heel, but after I land my triple toe loop, I feel invincible. Heels and all.

I launch off my skates to jump into my flying camel spin. By the time I move to my step sequence, I'm not even sure my skates are touching the ground anymore. It feels like I'm flying.

Except I'm not. I'm on the ice. I'm home. And I don't care what anyone thinks. Because I know that what I am doing is right. It's good.

And it should be enough.

Maybe there's applause when I finish skating. Maybe there isn't. I don't really care. I know I nailed it. Just like I planned to.

I want the perfection of the performance to carry me as I wait for the results, but I'm surprised when the joy of my time on the ice starts to fade. As I sit there staring at the screen, staring at Xander's name and hoping that mine shows up above his. Because even though I'm confident in my skate, the judges have the final say.

Finally, my score shows up on the screen, just below Ty's, bumping Xander's name to fourth. I blink. I'm proud. But I want to be . . . more. Elated. Thrilled. Losing-my-mind happy. I mean, I wish I had won outright. I always want to win. But I know that the technical elements of Ty's performance are simply worth more than mine. It doesn't matter how amazingly I skate; if the elements aren't there, I can't win.

And I skated amazingly. Like, super-duper incredibly amazingly.

I keep looking at my name above Xander's as some volunteers rush to set up a podium for the awards ceremony.

I did it. I beat him. I keep thinking those words over and over again. And when that doesn't feel like enough, I start adding mental exclamation points. *I did it! I beat him!*

Over and over, the words repeat. And slowly, I can feel my lips turning into a goofy smile. Maybe it's the fact that I've been nervous all day. That I've been unsure if I'd be allowed to even skate. It might be relief coupled with the stellar performance that has me giddy. It might be my own repeated mantra.

I did it! I beat him!

As I walk up to the makeshift podium, I scan the crowd to see if I can spot Xander and catch the look on his face. Most people have left for the day, but I find Heather. It's not hard to see her . . . or, it's not hard to hear her. She's screaming at the top of her lungs.

My feet are cased in my beat-up Converses instead of my white skates, and I'm bouncing once I get onto the small step for the silver medal. Sure, the guy standing in the bronze spot is a head taller than me. Who cares? I came out and skated like me, and it was enough to place!

From my perch on the podium, I brave a wave at Heather when it's announced that "Alex Smith" has won silver. It's not my name, but it's me. I won!

I'm not even mad at the text on my phone from Libby congratulating me. Even though I don't have it in me to respond, I don't have any room for anger after my win.

Heather offers to take me to Dairy Queen on the way home. It's a carryover from Dad, who would always take us for ice cream after any sort of competition or game. She runs off to the parking lot to pull the car around as I hunt down a single-stall bathroom to change in. I'm making my way to the parking lot when I'm attacked by a flying Libby.

"I'm sorry. I'm so so so so sorry."

I grunt a little, kind of taken aback by the force of this apology. "Okay," I say.

"Okay, you forgive me? Or okay, keep groveling?"

"The second before the first, I think. That was . . . it was really terrible," I say. I'm trying to find the right words, but *terrible* is the only one that even comes close.

"Mars, it was unbelievably terrible of me to do what I did," Libby agrees quickly. I nod. Agreeing with her agreement. "I'm really sorry. It's just . . ."

"Look. It hurt. That . . . whole thing. I didn't do anything to deserve that." I stop Libby as she's about to interrupt and apologize again. I need to make sure she hears me. Make sure she understands. "Rasha called me *it*." I flinch a little. The memory still hurts. "She did that to hurt me. She was looking right at me. That was awful. To be . . . basically told that I'm not some*one*, I'm some*thing*. And . . . look . . . people are gonna do that. People suck sometimes." I take a breath.

 129

"But my friends—my best friend—you can't just sit there and let someone do that to me. Because that's basically saying it's okay. Your friends don't have to like me. But they have to . . . treat me like a human. I can't . . . I can't do this alone. I can't be who I am in the world and have people I care about not sticking up for me. It's too hard."

To Libby's credit, she doesn't look away from me. And she doesn't try to interrupt again. She just listens. I take that to mean that I can keep going.

"It wasn't just about what your friends did. It's what *you* did. And look—" I swallow at this point. Because this next part . . . this is Libby's out. I don't want her to take it. I don't want us to stop being friends. But . . . I want to make sure she really *wants* to be my friend. "If you don't want to be friends . . . that . . . that sucks. A lot. But if that's what you want, tell me. Don't keep hurting me." My cheeks are hot. And I can feel the flush creeping down my neck.

Libby has been my best friend for as long as I can remember. But holding on to a friendship that's actually over doesn't sound like a good way to spend the next year of my life.

"I want to be your friend, Mars." She throws her arms around me and crushes me in a hug. I hug her back. We push the air out of each other's lungs until we both can't breathe anymore.

When we pull away, Libby is smiling. But I still need more. "And . . . ?" I prompt, hoping she understands.

"And . . . I have these other friends. I want these other friends."

"Even if they call me *it*?" I take a step away from Libby and wrap my arms around my torso. Because it hurts. Maybe Libby thinks she's being neutral, but that neutrality is hurting me. I'm bracing for impact, half expecting her to say that Rasha is more important to her than I am.

"And . . ." Libby bites her bottom lip. "I'm . . . gonna talk to Rasha. I was all wrapped up in wanting to have everything. Have you and have my new friends."

I look at Libby. I really want her to stick up for me. More than anything. I also don't want to be the reason she doesn't have any friends. The thought is an ugly one. Like I'm some kind of social toxin, polluting everyone I care about.

I almost think about backing down. For the first time in my life. Maybe it isn't worth wrecking Libby's life just to keep her as my friend.

I swallow. "What if Rasha doesn't want to be your friend anymore?" What if Libby has to choose?

"I don't want friends who can't respect others." They are good words, but they don't sound like Libby's.

"Did your moms talk to you?"

"Big-time." Libby wrinkles her nose a little. "A lot of talk about balance—you know the drill—but they're right. If Rasha wants to hang out with me, she can't rag on you. Even if . . ." Libby trails off.

Even if I make Rasha uncomfortable.

Even if she doesn't understand.

Even if no one else will challenge her.

I finish the sentence a million different ways in my head. Libby never does.

I decide to say the bravest thing I can think of. "You can have other friends, Libby."

"Yeah. It doesn't have to be either-or," she responds. Then she smiles and reaches her hand toward me.

"No," I say as I reach for her hand. "Maybe it doesn't have to be. I'm pretty anti-either-or. But . . . it can't be both if . . . Rasha . . ." My voice trails off. I think about the way it felt when Rasha called me *it*.

Libby's smile falters.

"If Rasha can't figure out how to treat me like a person . . ." I let the end of the sentence go. If Rasha keeps calling me *it*, I don't know if I will be able to stay friends with Libby if she stays friends with Rasha.

"Yeah, okay . . ." Libby nibbles at the skin on the edge of her finger.

It's not quite the reaction I want. It's something, and yet it's not enough. Still, Libby is my best friend. And even though a part of me considers walking away—just for a brief, horrible second—I push the thought away. I don't want to give up on her or us. Not yet.

After a long moment, she takes a breath and smiles. "Want

to talk about how you thrashed Xander? No eithers, ors, or buts about that!"

"I prefer soundly beat, but sure."

"I'm honestly a little nervous about tomorrow's practice. He's gonna be soooo sour."

"Are you really nervous?" I ask. I know we came up with this plan together, but I don't want to see Libby actually worried because I beat her partner.

"I just mean that he'll be in a bad mood. Whatever. Maybe he'll work a little harder."

"Maybe." I shrug. "Did you watch the whole comp?"

"Just the men's. Ty is something, huh? He's really great. Could have some serious potential."

"Could? I think definitely."

"Are you mad he beat you?" Libby asks.

"No." I say the word a little too fast, and Libby quirks her eyebrow. I definitely wanted to win outright, but getting silver to Ty's gold is okay. For now. "It's just good to know that if I want to keep up, I need to add some more technical elements." And just like that, the conversation feels good. Easy.

"Yeah . . . and take advantage of point accrual on the back half of your program and in your step sequences."

I grimace a little. There it is again, that Achilles' heel.

"It *was* you!" A deep voice rings out from the doorway.

I turn, and there Xander is. He's out of costume, in a pair of comfy sweats. I didn't see him in the stands. I thought he left.

He strides up and crosses his arms over his chest.

"I said I would beat you," I say simply, holding my ground.

"Just really thought you were a boy," Xander scoffs.

"Hey now," Libby says at almost the same time I say, "Maybe I am, maybe I'm not. The point is, I'm good enough to beat you."

"That's not the point. The point is you violated the rules. You intentionally lied on your paperwork. The MFSA is going to strip you of your medal."

"Excuse me?"

"Look. You aren't Alex Smith. There isn't an Alex Smith. Not one who skates, anyway. There's just Mars. Or whoever you are. And *she* isn't allowed to compete in the men's free skate."

The world blurs. This guy is a jerk. And what's worse, he *knows* he's being a jerk and is still *choosing* to be one.

"Well, whether I'm allowed to or not, I still got a better score than you. So it doesn't really matter what my gender is. The disagreement we had was about whether I could beat you, and I did."

"Wow. You really don't get it, do you? I thought that maybe you were just clueless. But you're a freak. And freaks don't get to compete."

It's Libby who steps up now. "What is wrong with you?" I'm thankful for her intervention, not just because it reinforces her apology from earlier, but because all I can imagine is balling up my fist and jamming it into Xander's eye. Or maybe his throat. And . . . I probably shouldn't do that.

"What's wrong with *me*?" Xander's voice is incredulous. "Libby, you're just a spoiled drama queen. I don't care how talented anyone thinks you are. It's not worth it."

"Excuse me? It's not my fault that you can't handle a little competition," Libby retorts.

"This partnership. It's done." Xander's voice is low. Then he twists away and stalks off.

Just then, the door to the rink opens and a flash of purple catches my eye. A bow perched on a high bun. Jade! She's hunched over her phone and typing furiously.

I wave.

"Hey, Jade."

I realize too late that I'm Alex Smith. Or I was when she saw me skate earlier.

"Hi." She looks up at me. Her eyes get a little wide. Then she looks over at Libby, then back at me. Her eyebrows draw together.

I take a breath and make a choice. "It's Mars," I say.

Libby looks back and forth between the two of us.

Jade's voice is flat when she says, "My brother was supposed to meet me here."

"Oh, we can wait with you . . . or." I take a step toward her, and she counters, moving away from me almost defensively. "Do you . . ." I want to offer her a ride. I'm pretty sure Heather wouldn't mind an extra stop on the way home.

"No. I just have to wait."

"Okay."

It's weird, but after writing back and forth with Jade so much, this conversation is . . . disappointing. Jade seems distracted. Maybe even grouchy. What gives?

I grab Libby's arm and bring her closer to Jade.

"This is Libby," I say. Smiling.

"Hi!" Libby says.

Jade doesn't say anything. She just looks back at her phone.

"Um, look," I say, "maybe it's none of my business, but you seem off."

"You don't really know me that well, Mars. Just like I don't know you."

Her words are clipped, and they sting a little. My heartbeat kicks up a notch. That happens around Jade. Almost always. But it's different this time. There's an edge. Normally, I want to do everything in my power to stay around her. Now? I want to run.

But Dad was right. I don't walk away. And it's basically impossible for me to let things go.

"Okay. Hi, I'm Mars. I'm twelve years old, and I like to skate. A lot."

Libby catches on. "Hi, I'm Libby. I'm thirteen and also a skater, though I just started doing pairs."

Jade looks up. "Yeah. I know. You're my brother's partner."

CHAPTER 15

I don't remember the ride home.

All I really remember is pulling out my phone and checking Instagram. But Jade hasn't posted something new. And she hasn't written to me.

Her awkwardness wasn't about my stint as Alex Smith at the Snow Ball. It's because of something worse.

Xander is Jade's brother.

I scroll back in time and look at the pictures of her on her brother's shoulders at the lake. In the background, there's a blurry face obscured by a splash of water, but I'm almost positive it's Xander. As I keep scrolling, I see more evidence of him. A hand in the picture with the marshmallows, I'm sure that's his. The photo of her looking out the window. Did Xander take it?

I think about writing to her. Maybe a dozen times. I start messages.

How long did you know?
Are you mad at me?

I'm mad . . .

I'm not mad at you . . .

Your bro kinda sucks . . .

I'm sorry I lied . . .

I don't send any of them.

Just then, a new update shows up. Jade has posted a picture of herself midspin. Her skates are moving so fast they blur a bit. The caption reads: **Great day on the ice. But then every day on the ice is great.**

Mom gets Indian food for dinner. Heather and I both dig in. In no time, our plates are piled with chicken tikka masala and saag paneer, and we're just eating silently . . . until Mom asks how practice went. Heather gives a wide smile, and I kick her under the table.

"Did you talk to that girl again?" Mom asks.

"What girl? There's a girl?" Heather's interest is piqued.

"No and no."

"Mars met a girl during their skates in Detroit. She seems nice," Mom says as she reaches for a samosa.

"She *is* nice," I say. Or she was. Until she found out I lied to her.

"So, when you said no and no, what you meant was no and yes." Heather's smile is ginormous and annoying.

"I meant no, and there is no girl in the way both of you are insinuating. She's a friend. End of story."

"Okay," Mom says, and I relax a little.

"Was she at the rink today?" Heather asks, and my shoulders tense up again.

I roll my eyes. "Yes."

"What color was she wearing?"

"Purple," I say. I kind of grind the word between my teeth. This conversation? This is the worst. I thought talking about dead dads or coming out as nonbinary was bad . . . Talking about the girl I have a crush on and who has *just* revealed that she is related to my rival . . . that is approximately fifty-two times worse.

Heather nods mischievously. Ugh. She sucks when she's like this.

"She does seem nice . . . ," Heather says. Her voice kind of sings the word *nice*.

"Oh, did you watch the practice?" Mom asks. "Usually, you just hunt down a coffee shop and do homework." My eyes widen slightly. I don't want Heather to blow my cover.

"Yeah," says Heather. "I just wanted to see how V's doing. I've been missing her practices. Seems she hasn't been missing *me* though."

Her. She. V. Those words prick. Dig in a way that Heather isn't even aware of.

But it isn't her misgendering language that sets me off. The real issue is the casual way Heather's talking about me *liking* someone.

I barely feel comfortable having a crush in the first place. And listening to my sister and my mom *talk* about it—no, *joke* about it—is infuriating. To top it off, I'm pretty sure that Jade hates me now, so their cheeriness about my potential crush feels even more cruel. I jump up from the table, grab a piece of naan, and shove it into my mouth.

"I'm done eating. I'm excusing myself. Leave me alone!" I yell, my mouth overflowing with starch. I pick up my plate and bring it to the kitchen, where I dump it in the sink. Hard. The whole plate shatters. Clumps of orange sauce run between the jagged cracks of the plate.

"Mars . . . ," Mom says, her voice lower than normal.

Maybe it's a warning voice. Maybe it's the kind of voice you would use with a frightened dog that's gone wild. I don't really know. And I don't really care.

"Leave me alone!" I scream, my voice bubbling out of my throat in a shrill, broken way. The world shifts a little. Everything is kind of blurry. People say that they see red when they get mad, but apparently, I don't. I see everything as though I'm in the middle of a spin, all of the colors flowing into one another to make a muddy mess.

I half run, half stumble up the stairs to my bedroom. I grab Dad's Michigan sweatshirt from the dresser, pull it up to my face, shove it into my mouth, and scream. Hard.

I let myself cry for a while then. Everything hurts. My body is sore from a week of intense practices and the tension of competition. And from lying.

From trying to be something I'm not.

All the time.

 140

I put Dad's sweatshirt on and pull my arms in through the sleeves, wrap them around my torso, and just let the fabric flop around and cocoon me. I'm a blob. A shapeless being that's just feeling. I'm not a girl. Not a boy. Not even really a person. Just feelings.

It's late when I finally move again. My knees are stiff from being bent and swallowed in Dad's sweatshirt.

When I go back to the kitchen, the sink is empty. Mom has already efficiently swept away the debris from my outburst and is nestled in the corner of the couch in the living room, flipping through a magazine. Heather is doing homework at the kitchen table and making it a point not to notice me.

"Sorry," I mumble. I'm not sure if I mean it. But I know it's what I'm supposed to say.

"It's . . ." Mom pauses as she puts down the magazine and gestures for me to come sit with her. She waits for me to sit and then says, "Well, I was going to say, it's okay. And I would rather it wasn't. But we get it. Heather and I aren't going to tease you."

"Not yet, anyway," Heather adds in. She still doesn't look up from her homework.

"That sounds an awful lot like teasing, Heather," I warn.

She finally looks up. "Chuck a plate at my head. Mom might have to be the bigger person, but I'm your sister. I get to be a pain sometimes."

"Okay," I say. My voice is a little rough.

"And you're not the only one who's hurting," Heather adds, standing up and walking toward the couch.

"Heather . . ." There's a warning in Mom's voice.

"No. She—*they* don't get to act like this is only their pain." Heather flops down to sit next to me. "I get it. There's other stuff happening for you, Mars. But we're all hurting. And there's stuff happening for all of us. We're all . . . trying. And . . . it's not okay. It really, really sucks. But you aren't the only one who lost someone. You aren't the only one going through stuff."

I blink.

Heather and I never really talk about Dad.

I mean, I know she misses him . . . but it's hard to see. Or hear. Or even really know.

Over the summer, she was always locked away in her room, listening to records. Or working on her computer. How am I supposed to know she's . . . well, dealing with it in her own way?

After the conversation, I go back to my room and just kind of hang out, numbly scrolling through my phone. I think about what Heather said as I look at all of the pictures of people smiling. Each of them, no matter what they look like in that photo, has other stuff going on. Grief. Anger. Confusion. Maybe even joy?

It's past midnight when I finally drift off to sleep.

I have weird dreams. Dreams where I'm at a competition, but my ice time keeps getting pushed back. It's unclear why—if the tournament is running slow or it's some kind of dream logic. I'm not allowed to sit in the bleachers. Each time I try to sneak in to watch the other skaters, someone catches me. "No. You have to wait your turn." I can't quite make out the face of the bleacher guard. But every so often there's a gasp from the crowd or a fit of cheers, and I wonder what's going on out there. Finally, Jade comes and grabs me and shoves me on the ice. I skate. I'm wearing a leotard and tights. Nothing else. My body feels cold and really exposed. I go to skate, but my skates are heavy. And they aren't working like normal skates. I can't pick my feet up off the ice. I keep going, but every time I try to jump, my foot sticks to the ice, like there's a magnet holding it down. I keep skating. I keep not jumping. The program continues. The music goes on and on. I just keep skating.

My alarm doesn't wake me up. It's Mom.

"Mars, you're going to be late to school."

I bolt out of bed and grab my phone. It's Monday. It's morning. The sun is up. I'm supposed to be at practice! I grab my skating bag and start to figure out what I have that I can wear.

"You slept through your practice." Mom's voice halts my movement.

"You let me sleep through my practice?" My tone is sharp. Panicked. I need practice. And Jade might be at practice today. Maybe we could—I don't know. Talk?

"Honey, you were out. I just . . . I couldn't do it. I called Katya. We can reschedule."

"No, I have to . . ."

"School starts in fifteen minutes. I can call you in sick if you want, but if you do that, no skating."

"No! I'll go," I say. I throw on clothes, and Mom drives me to school. I'm just a few minutes late to Ms. Char's class.

She gives me a wave but doesn't make a big deal of me being late. I think about what other teachers might do. Imagine Mr. Zoroski, who would inevitably say something like, *Thank you for joining us, Veronica,* which is just the worst.

When I get to my desk, I slump and put my head down on the table. Man, I'm tired. Ms. Char doesn't call on me, but she does ask me to stay back after class.

"Hey, Mars. Just checking in." Ms. Char pushes two desks together and takes a seat in one of them. She indicates that I should sit across from her.

I don't. I really hope this conversation doesn't last long.

"Uh, yeah. I'm . . . I just overslept." I shift my weight from foot to foot.

"Do you have your paragraph?" she asks with a smile.

"What?" I genuinely don't know what she's talking about.

"Over the weekend, you were researching someone we've never heard of that made a lasting impact on society. Remember?"

No. I don't remember.

"Uh . . ." I think wildly about what I can say or how I can cover.

"Look, I'm going to contact your mom. Just to let her

144

know that you've fallen behind on the work. Maybe she can remind you about the assignment. I told you I would give you a warning before I wrote home with your name, so I want to ask what you would like me to call you in my email . . ." Ms. Char stands up now and gives me a questioning look.

I'm a little relieved that we are talking about my name and not my assignment. "Uh, yeah, Mom calls me Mars now."

"Okay. Good. I'm glad to hear that." She seems genuinely happy about it.

"Yeah," I say.

"Do you think you can get the paragraph done tonight?" Ms. Char asks.

Tonight? I hope I get to skate tonight.

"Maybe," I hedge.

"'Cause it's overdue now. I don't take points off for it being late, but it's just going to sit there and pile up."

"No, I get it," I say quickly. Can this conversation just be done now?

"And I usually let parents know when that happens."

"I get it," I repeat.

"You're taking this pretty well." Ms. Char smiles.

"Yeah," I say. Because what else am I supposed to say?

After a pause, Ms. Char says, "Okay, well, I'm going to let your mom know. And . . . Mars? Let me know if you need some other support."

"Okay."

I'm not sure what she means by "other support." Probably

another meeting with Mrs. Hearse, the school counselor. I need that like I need a dislocated shoulder.

The rest of school trudges on. During attendance, Mr. Rojos calls me Veronica. I think about correcting him. About asking him to call me Mars. But I don't. I'm really tired.

One good thing is that Libby sits with me at lunch. She doesn't question my silence, just babbles on about the day. It's nice.

After school, I'm still dragging. But I'm unwilling to miss free skate at Four Corners, especially since I missed ice time this morning.

I'm a little slow packing up my bag and changing into skating clothes.

I hear when Mom comes home. The door opens and she plops her keys in the shell we bought on a vacation to Sanibel Island. And then her coat comes off and the closet opens. I hope she remembers I have skating.

"Hey, Mars?" she calls out.

"Yeah," I say. I stretch the word out so there are about five vowel sounds in it.

"Can you come to the living room?"

"Sure," I say.

I slip on my clogs, throw my skating bag over my shoulder, and march out to the living room. Mom's sitting on the couch.

"Can you take a seat?"

"Uh, yeah." Mom's face is pinched, and I instinctively move slowly as I make my way to the armchair. This doesn't seem like it's going to be a *Let's both sit on the couch together* conversation.

"I got an email from one of your teachers today. Ms. Char." I let out a breath. Okay, I knew this was coming. I can handle this.

"Yeah," I say. "She said she was gonna write to you."

"You missed an assignment." Mom's voice is low now. And quiet. We've never had a conversation like this. So formal and . . . distant. But then, I've never missed an assignment before. This is a new Without Dad development.

"It's just a paragraph. I'll get it done," I say. There's a part of me that wants to roll my eyes, but I keep it in check.

"Before skating."

No! "Free skate starts in twenty minutes!" I can feel my voice getting whiny, almost begging Mom to reconsider.

"Then I guess you'll be motivated to finish your overdue work," Mom says simply.

"Ugh!" I jump up from the chair and ball up my fists.

"Don't say this isn't fair. It *is* fair." She stays seated and maddeningly calm.

"Fine. It's annoying," I concede, pushing out each sound of the words with precision.

"Okay."

I'm over this. I'm over calm Mom and being late for skating

and writing school paragraphs and all of it. I go to leave the living room. To grab my computer so I can type something. Anything.

"She mentioned something else," Mom calls after me.

"What?" I freeze.

"She said that you seemed down. Out of it. She said that she was glad that you opened up about your name, but that ever since then, she noticed that you've been quiet."

There's more. I can tell there's more. "And . . . ?"

"And that isn't like you."

"Maybe she doesn't know me very well," I say. Echoing the words that Jade said after the competition yesterday. Maybe none of us knows anyone.

Mom softens a little then. She stands and moves toward me. "Don't get mad. She's looking out for you. *I'm* looking out for you."

"I'm not mad," I say, shrugging away when she reaches to put a hand on my shoulder.

"Okay." Mom says it in that way that says she doesn't believe me. I don't really care if she believes me.

"Can I go now?" I ask, but I'm already walking to my room. "I need to do this assignment."

"Do you want me to talk to the school about changing your name on their records?" The words come out in a rush, like Mom's been thinking about saying them for a long time, and they just burst out of her.

I freeze again. "What?" I ask.

"Do you want me to talk to the school about changing your name to Mars? About making sure they know and use your pronouns?"

"That's a formal way of asking." I don't look at her.

"Well, it's not a conversation I've had before. I did a little internet research. Do you?"

Do I?

I don't know. In some ways, yes. It would be nice if I didn't have to tense every time a teacher called me Veronica. Or cringe whenever I overheard someone referring to me as "she." But officially changing who I am? Going to the school and making a thing out of it? I'm not sure that's what I want right now either.

"You can think about it," Mom says finally.

I nod.

"Maybe while you write your paragraph."

CHAPTER 16

I can't really get going on my paragraph. I know that I could just write something, anything really, and be done with it.

Instead, I keep thinking about how Ms. Char has been so kind. And I don't really want to just throw together some crappy sentences. I want to do something thoughtful.

I also want to skate.

So I make a silent promise to do a better version of the assignment later, type up some nonsense, and run out to the living room, holding my computer up to Mom.

"Done! Can we go skating now?"

"Yes," Mom says. She already has her coat on, so we're out the door in less than a minute.

Mom still seems kind of tense as she drives to the ice rink. I try to ignore it, but she's squeezing the steering wheel tight. Instead of pulling up to the door, she parks.

"You're, uh, coming in?" I say.

"Yes."

"You're not gonna go get a coffee or something?"

"No."

"Okay."

Mom trails me in. Sticks close. The rink is light tonight. Not many people are skating. Mom stays next to me as I sit and pull on my skates.

"Are they getting small?" she asks. "I think you might be growing."

"Uh . . ." I try to think. I'm not sure. I haven't really noticed. Yes, my skates are a little tight, but I always chalk that up to the fact that I tie them as tight as I possibly can. Sometimes, I even pause in the middle of a practice to get them tighter.

"What size are those?"

"Fives," I say.

"Okay, we can get some new ones soon."

I furrow my brow a little. Mom's definitely acting weird.

"Can I see your program? The one you've been working on with Katya and Dmitri?"

"Uh, sure."

I wait for her to turn and walk to sit in the stands, but she doesn't.

"I'm not going to the bleachers."

Okaaaaay . . .

Mom walks to the door with me. I'm half convinced she's going to walk on the ice in her flats. She doesn't though. She just leans against the rink wall.

"I don't have my music," I say.

"That's okay. I just want to see what you've been working on."

"Okay."

I move through my warm-up, like normal. Work my way up to the triple. I'm still not feeling one hundred percent, but I try to shake it off. I land my triple in warm-up, so I figure I might as well run through the routine.

I move to center ice.

There are a few other skaters, but everyone seems pretty chill. Absorbed in their own work.

I close my eyes and take a deep breath, imagining the competition yesterday. Thinking about everything that's happened since then. Libby coming back. Jade going away. The fight with Xander. My conversation with Ms. Char. As I think about each thing, each moment, I let it fall away. Try to just focus on how great it felt to skate yesterday. Just me and the ice. That's all I need right now.

In my mind, I imagine I can hear the vocals of my program music. I imagine the instruments coming in along with the insistent words. A few lines in, I hit the triple. Or at least I thought I would, but I spring into it too aggressively. Too hard. I bend my knee too much. And I over-rotate. Maybe a quarter too far. But it's enough to mess up my landing and send me slamming to the ice.

It gets quiet then. Maybe Mom gasps. Maybe the few other skaters are looking at me.

I think about watching Jade on the ice. Watching her fall so early in her program on that double axel.

And I think about how she got up and just kept skating.

Didn't just keep skating. She excelled. She didn't let the fall keep her from delivering.

So I get up. Take a breath and let the song come back into my head.

I skate into my next move, a spin, and I keep going.

I'm pretty sure everyone saw me fall, because all attention is on me now. I don't have to mind their spaces, because they quickly skate out of the way when I move to their corners of the ice.

I get through the rest of the program.

I don't smile like Jade did, but I push through. I make sure that the rest of the run of the routine isn't wasted. I end the skate, hitting my final pose and holding it just like I did in the competition yesterday. I hear the dull thud of Mom clapping through her mittens. I skate over and lean on the boards. She's got her arms wide. Holding them out for a hug.

"Sorry I messed up," I say.

"It's good to know you're human," she whispers back. "And it's good to know you can keep going when things are tough. That was incredible."

I'm not sure why, but I kind of feel like crying then. It's hard to describe.

Mom gives me another squeeze.

"What are you going to do with the rest of your time tonight? Work on that triple?"

I think for a second. "No. I've gotta solidify my twizzles."

"Okay. I'll be here." She backs up from the boards but stays rink-side and sits down.

I skate back out and start working through the sequence that Katya showed me at our last lesson. Throughout the rest of the practice, Mom keeps looking at her phone. Not to scroll through it like Heather would, but like she's expecting a call or something.

I try to focus on my twizzles. They're not smooth at first. Takes time. I keep going, over and over. I wish that Jade were here. She's good at this stuff. And even if I'm not doing it well, it would be fun to smile with her.

Then I think about our last conversation.

Her brother.

Her brother is Xander.

I keep skating. Pushing through. Pushing thoughts of Jade out of my head. I just need to keep skating. Keep working. I don't need to think about Jade right now. I just need to think about skating.

Mom's looking at her phone again when my time on the ice ends.

"You expecting someone to call?" I ask.

She startles a little. Then says, "Yes. I am. I talked to Katya this morning when I called to let her know you weren't able to come to your session, and I'm waiting on a follow-up call."

"A follow-up? About what?"

Just then, Mom's phone rings. We both jump, but she answers it.

"Hello? . . . Yes, this is she . . . Yes. That's my child . . . No, not my daughter . . . No, not my son."

I listen intently. It's clear Mom's talking about me. There's a long pause as she listens to the phone. She's breathing loudly through her nose, and I wonder if the person on the other end can hear it. When Mom talks again, her voice is louder than it was before. It isn't a yell, exactly. It's a little more controlled than that. A little more dangerous.

"Well, I just don't see how that is fair. My child earned the score that got h—them second place, did they not?" The other person answers, and my head is spinning, imagining what they're saying. Mom is continuing on, "Can you give me the number for the regional office? . . . Well, if you don't want me to take it to the regional office, you can leave the results as they stand."

There's another pause. Then Mom's voice gets quiet. "Okay. Well, I'm sure we'll be in touch."

I know Mom has been mad before, but I've never seen her look it. Until now. Now she's clutching her fists and working to control her breathing. It's clear that she's furious.

"Mars, did you compete yesterday?" she finally asks.

I think about lying. And I hate that I think it. Because what would I say? That there's been a misunderstanding? That people just thought it was me? But she already knows the truth. She just didn't hear it from me.

"Yeah." I hang my head. Sure, I didn't want to tell her, but I didn't want her to find out this way either.

"And you placed second in the men's division?"

"Yes." Part of me wants to tag on an, *Isn't that kind of impressive, at least?*

"Okay. Well, the Michigan Figure Skating Association is conducting an investigation into your participation in the competition." Her words are detached. Clinical.

I blink. Are they taking away my medal? Are they going to tell everyone I'm a fraud? Are they going to ban me from skating for life? "What does that mean?" I finally ask.

"I don't know yet."

My head swims a little as those words settle around me. Everything has gone horribly wrong.

Mom's phone rings again, and she answers it, her voice still holding on to some of the anger from her last call. I'm not paying attention to what she's saying this time. The conversation doesn't last long, less than a minute. My head still feels odd when Mom explains it was a reporter. An article about all this is going to come out tomorrow.

Great. Not only did I make a big mistake . . . now everyone gets to know about it.

CHAPTER 17

M om earned her law degree when Heather was a baby. It's something I sometimes forget because she doesn't work as a lawyer. But it's like this superpower that she can activate when she needs to sign a contract or negotiate with someone.

Or when she has to fight for her child to keep their second place at the Snow Ball.

It's Tuesday when the article comes out online on *Southeast Michigan Live*. I get approximately twenty texts at once linking to it. I didn't even know that many people had my number. The *SML* article describes the Snow Ball. How the last skater was small and unassuming in white skates and how that skater landed a triple in the opening of the program and continued impressing the crowd after that.

There's a quote from Ty, saying how he had never met the skater before, but that he seemed nice enough. And really talented.

And then the article turns.

Coming into a new competition circuit and claiming silver is enough of a story. But, as Xander Shen shares, there's more. Alex Smith isn't Alex Smith at all.

"Her name is Veronica Hart. Sometimes she goes by Mars. Not only is she a girl, she's twelve. That makes her ineligible to compete in the division on two counts."

Shen has an interest in seeing Hart stripped of her medal. He missed the podium by one, placing fourth, and a bronze would strengthen his bid for future competitions. Shen has been skating for almost ten years.

"I love the sport. It's frustrating to see people violating the rules."

While Hart's skills as a skater aren't in question, whether the rule violation will strip her of her silver medal is. All eyes are on the Michigan Figure Skating Association, which has the task of determining whether Hart's win is legitimate.

"We haven't made a ruling yet," says MFSA president Charlie Roderique. "It's a complicated situation. The rules exist for a reason."

Hart declined to comment.

I hate the article. I hate that it keeps calling me "she." And I hate that it makes Xander seem like some kind of reasonable skating advocate and not a prejudiced jerk.

On Wednesday, Mom drives me to skating in Detroit.

"I want to talk to Katya and Dmitri before you work with them," she says as I go to put my skates on. I scan the lobby, and I'm not sure, but I have this weird feeling that everyone is looking at me.

I don't have my skates laced up all the way when Mom comes back.

"We're leaving. You can take off your skates in the car."

I go to argue, but Mom's got my arm in a vise grip, and we're moving toward the door. I'm barely able to grab my bag.

Mom gets in the van without saying anything, pushes a CD into the CD player, and turns up the music.

"Panic in Detroit" comes blaring out of the speakers.

So I'm guessing the conversation didn't go well.

I don't say anything as Mom drives home. I spend a little time thinking about what might have happened back at the rink, but soon Bowie's voice is taking over my thoughts. Just like it always did when Dad came home and insisted that we all have a dance party.

And then, I'm missing Dad. Missing having another person to lean on. Another person in my corner. Missing his corny jokes. Missing the way that he could make Mom laugh when no one else could. Missing his beard. Missing the moment when he shaved his beard, and we all screamed. I'm just an aching pit of missing.

When we get home, Mom turns to me.

"You don't have to go to school if you don't want to."

"I don't want to," I say.

"Okay."

I finally shore up my courage and ask: "What did they say?"

"They said you're talented, but there isn't a competitive path for you as something other than a girl. That even if the MFSA doesn't strip you of the silver, there are just going to be continued battles about your legitimacy in competition. And they have to focus their time on prospects that have a clearer path to higher-level competitions."

There isn't a path for you as something other than a girl.

That hurts.

Being told that there isn't a space for me in the world that I love. It's a punch to the gut.

I've skated since I was four. Since before I knew that being a girl was something that didn't quite fit. Before I figured out that I was nonbinary, I figured out I was a skater. And now I'm being told that I can't be that.

"So if I want to keep skating, I have to be a girl."

"No."

"That's what they said," I press. I love my mom. Love that she is going to fight to make space for me in the world. But I want to know what we're up against.

"That is what they said. It's their opinion."

"Yeah, but they're—I mean, we hired them for their opinion."

Mom doesn't say anything.

And all I can think is I know Dad thought I was brave.

 160

But maybe I'm not brave enough to spend my whole life fighting. Maybe I'm not Achilles.

Or maybe I am, and my heel is something no one expected.

On Thursday, the MFSA calls Mom to say that they're stripping me of second place. That they have to honor the rules put in place by the governing body.

They say I can hold on to the medal as a keepsake, but that Alex Smith will be expunged from all records.

I can hold on to the medal as a keepsake.

What a joke.

Like I want to remember anything about this horrible week.

The week I lost my win, my coach, and my crush.

Mom lets me stay home from school again. And at least I still have Libby, who calls me about once an hour, even from school. I don't answer, but it's nice to know that she's thinking of me. I text her to tell her that I appreciate her calls, but I'm not ready to talk yet.

> Libby: I'll keep calling
> Libby: Answer when ur ready

Mom spends most of the day on the phone, talking through how she can appeal the decision and discussing with some of her lawyer friends whether it's worth bringing in the press on this conversation.

I just keep thinking about what Katya and Dmitri said. About how there is no path for me as a skater if I'm not a girl.

And I'm not a girl.

It might be that accepting this part of me—the insistent part that says over and over that I'm not a girl and not a boy—is too at odds with the world. That the system isn't built to be nonbinary.

We're at odds. Skating and me. And maybe, to keep skating, I need to let go of the enby part of me. I need to be okay with learning to skate delicately and wearing sparkly skirts. I need to be okay with hiding who I am so I can do what I love.

Or what I used to love.

I'm not so sure anymore.

Is skating worth smothering that part of me? Or is that part of me worth giving up skating?

I flop back on the bed and try to imagine not skating again. Not spinning. Not leaping. Not improving my footwork. It's hard. It hurts to imagine life that way.

Then I try imagining going through the world with more articles calling me "she." Staying Veronica. And that thought is unbearable. It makes my skin want to shift over my bones.

So that's my answer.

I think about throwing the medal in the trash, but that doesn't seem final enough. Because it will sit in my trash can until our cleaning person comes and moves it to the big trash. And then it will sit there until trash day. It will just linger. Moving from one trash can to another.

And I don't want any of this to linger in my life.

I want to be done.

So I put my skates and the medal in a canvas bag and take a walk. I wave to Mom as I go, and she pulls the phone from her ear. "Are you okay? Where are you going?"

No. I'm not okay. "Just for a walk. To clear my head."

"Okay."

Maybe she doesn't notice the bag on my shoulder. Maybe she does. I'm not sure. I go out the front door, my feet stepping one in front of the other without thought. I know where I'm headed. To the woods at the end of the block. And once I get there, I go even deeper. Deeper and deeper. Until the woods open up to the small pond.

Dad's and my winter skating spot.

There's a little algae covering the top of the pond. The surface looks still and peaceful.

I stand for a while just looking. Being still and watching the pond. The dragonflies and turtles going about their business. I never came here with Dad when the pond wasn't frozen.

Sorry to ruin your peace, I think.

Then I reach into the bag.

I start with the medal. I swing back my arm and heave it into the middle of the pond. It lands with a *plop* and takes a chunk of algae down to the bottom of the pond with it.

Next, my left skate. I grab the blade and swing the boot like I'm heaving a hammer at the Olympics. The splash is huge, and a duck flaps out of the pond in distress. Then I pull out the other skate. I walk around the edge of the pond and find another chunk of undisturbed algae. I try not to think too hard as I chuck the right boot into the water.

I wait until the ripples settle. Until everything goes back to its own peaceful rhythm.

Soon, I can barely tell that I've thrown my skates away.

CHAPTER 18

The only thing I can think to do at this point is allow Dad's sweatshirt to swallow me whole. I try to keep from crying by looking at all of the small details on the sweatshirt. The pizza stain from his first date with Mom—when she supposedly broke down crying because she had just had a bad day at work. The collar has almost completely dislocated from the rest of the sweatshirt. Mom offered to fix that—well, she offered to get it fixed, because she said her approaching anything with a needle and thread is dangerous—but I don't want her to. I just want the sweatshirt to be. Maybe it can stay and just keep that small bit of Dad smell alive.

It's not really working. The whole focusing on the details and not crying thing. Soon, tears are streaming down my cheeks and my breath is uneven and loud. I pull my head into the chest of the sweatshirt, which only seems to amplify the sound of my sniffles. I can still see the light from my bedroom through the parts of Dad's sweatshirt that are worn through, but I curl up and imagine that the sweatshirt can keep the world from getting at me.

But Mom does. Get at me.

I'm just about to fall asleep when she quietly opens the door.

"Mars?" Mom's voice is soft. Hushed. Maybe even kind.

I pull the sweatshirt tighter around me.

"Mars, you don't have to talk about what happened at the competition if you don't want to. Not now. I think I have a pretty good idea from the skating association. But whenever you feel up to it, I would really like to hear your side of the story."

My side? I don't even know what my side is anymore.

I burrow deeper.

"Okay. No talking from you yet. Well, can I just sit here? And maybe ramble on a little?"

I don't say yes. But I don't say no either.

"Mars, I remember your first competition. Do you remember it?"

I don't say anything, but I do remember. I still have the skating costume in my closet. A small hyper-colored leo and skirt combo that looks like it was splattered with paint. I thought I was so cool.

"You probably don't remember it the way I do."

Mom's hand is worming its way around my shoulders, and I can feel her pulling me into her lap. I keep my eyes closed and just listen.

"I was really nervous. Your dad told me you would be fine a hundred times between our house and the rink. But we got to the competition, and your coach, Sharon—maybe you don't remember her. Well, anyway, she didn't show up. She just wasn't there. And I was furious. Dad was mad too, but he kept his cool, and just rolled up his sleeves and said that he was your coach at registration. And you . . . you just smiled and went along with it. You wanted to compete so badly. You weren't going to let something silly like a no-show coach stop you from showing what you could do.

"You drew first and had to skate right after the Zamboni cleaned the ice. I remember looking at your tiny reflection on that smooth ice when you skated out and took your opening position, and I remember thinking: *How can they do this? They're only seven.* And your dad wasn't there in the stands with me to tell me that you could. So I just sat there picking at my fingers. Just like you pick at your fingers."

She pulls out one of my hands and starts to rub over my worried nail beds, reminding me that we're related. I think about Heather's hands too. Worry-worn just like mine. Even though I've been obsessing over what's different about me, there's so much of us that is alike.

"Your music started. It was some classical piece."

"*The Nutcracker,*" I whisper.

"Yes, *The Nutcracker.* You started and right away you were supposed to go into a spin. And you fell. Just *bam.* Right down on your butt. I watched the rest of the program through my fingers. And you did fine. You got up and made up the ground as best you could.

"And then the other skaters came. I wanted to murder

167

your coach all over again because those other girls were so clearly more experienced and more, well, just *more* than you. And I thought: *This is it. My kid finds something they love, and we're going to crush that love with competition. This is how it ends.*"

My heart lightens when Mom says the word *they*. Maybe she's trying hard to get my pronouns right. Maybe it just happened. Whatever the reason, I sink a little deeper into her embrace.

Mom's right. I don't remember all of this. I remember falling. I remember being embarrassed. And I remember thinking, *I'm not going to do that again.* And I didn't. I don't remember the other skaters though. I'm lost in my own memory for a moment, but Mom's voice pulls me back.

"—your dad and I saw the scores before you did. Knew you had gotten last. You had already fallen; did they really need to crush your dreams twice? But everyone went rushing to the score postings, and you got caught up in the scuffle, and before I could grab you and lie about how they were going to mail the scores or something, you were there and back. A huge smile plastered across your face."

Mom smiles and imitates my little kid voice. "'Mom! Dad! There were three judges and one of them gave me sixth! One didn't think I was the worst!'" She chuckles a little then. "You were so excited that one person didn't think you were the worst. I don't know if that judge took pity on you or was the only one who saw some of your grit and potential. I don't really care. I was just thankful that I got to spend the after-noon with my kid, who was thrilled to come in seventh out of seven."

Seventh out of seven. Pathetic.

"And I know what you're thinking. Seventh out of seven. That sounds bad. But that was the thing, kiddo. For you, in the moment, it really wasn't. That's who you are. In that moment, you found some kind of motivation. And that drive. That made you happy. That belief that you had a place in the world of skating. That was something."

I take a deep breath. She's right. Until this week, I thought of the ice as home. I thought there was a place for me in fig-ure skating. That's what makes this whole thing feel worse. Like a betrayal.

"You kept training. Pushing. You insisted that every time you fell in practice was one less time you would fall in com-petition. You asked for more practice and more ice time. That was the first thing on every birthday list."

I sniff and wipe my eyes. "Guess I have to think of some-thing new to want for my birthday," I say with a weak chuckle. Mom laughs too. But then I'm crying again. "I'm done, Mom. I threw my skates in the pond."

"Oh, Mars . . . ," Mom says. She presses my head into the hollow of her neck. I cry and cry, and she just holds me. We go on like that, just crying and holding.

I'm finally breathing a little easier when she pulls away to look me in the eyes.

"Look, if you want to stop skating because you want to do other things, or because competition isn't doing it for you anymore, that's fine. But not wanting to do it because you think you don't belong on the ice? That's ridiculous. Skating is who you are. Just like being nonbinary is who you are. And my job as your mom is to help you figure out who you are and make sure that the world makes space for you."

I meet Mom's gaze. Maybe I don't want to quit skating. But I don't want to pretend to be someone else to keep doing what I love. Why does everything have to be so confusing?

"Did I really not get that seventh place was bad?" I finally ask.

"Maybe you did. Maybe you didn't. It doesn't really matter. It didn't break you. Just like this isn't going to break you."

I use the sleeve of Dad's sweatshirt to wipe my nose.

"So, if I still want to compete . . . ," I whisper, thinking about my skates at the bottom of the pond.

"If that's what you want to do, we'll figure out how you can do it. Not by lying. By making our voices heard."

"I don't even know what to say." My voice is a squeak, next to nothing.

"Well, I'm sure you can figure it out."

I wish I had Mom's confidence in me.

CHAPTER 19

The next morning, there's a pair of black skates with a massive purple bow on them on the dining room table.

"What are these?" I ask.

"I hope you know what skates are . . . ," Heather says, teasing.

"Yeah, but . . ."

"You can choose to break them in or not. Whatever you want, Mars," Mom says. Then she leans in and presses a kiss to my forehead. "But the hockey team is playing away tonight, so I've booked an hour of ice time at Four Corners at six. You can skate or not."

"Okay."

"For what it's worth, you should probably skate," Heather says.

"No. It's Mars's choice."

Heather looks down at her book and says, "Yeah, sure," under her breath.

I take out my phone and open Instagram to look for a

message from Jade. It took less than a week, but it's a habit now. Just to check. She's the only person I follow. Since the Snow Ball, Jade has only posted competition pictures with quotes for captions, no original content. No secret messages about how she's having a massive disagreement with a family member because he's being a jerk to a little enby skater who beat him.

I pull up our messages. We haven't written to each other since the competition.

I sigh.

She said I didn't know her. That we didn't know each other.

But maybe . . . maybe I still *want* to know Jade. And maybe if that's going to happen, I need to make the first move. Dad said I was brave. Well, typing in this app feels like the bravest thing I can do right now.

> **@SkatingOn*Mars*: Hey. I know things are messed up. But hi. My name is Mars. I love to skate. I love to compete. I'm also nonbinary. I only just am out about it though. So I'm not good at telling people. Or explaining. So I told a lie. I told a lie so I could skate against a boy who dared me. And that boy happens to be your brother. If you want to hear the**

**rest, if you want to know my side of the
story, just come to Four Corners at 6pm.
I hope I see you there.**

I close the app then and pull up Libby's contact info. The phone rings a couple of times.

"Mars! I'm so glad you called. I'm sorry. I'm sorry about getting you to do that competition. MFSA is so out of it. I can't believe they're doing what they're doing. Neither can my moms. Honestly, we might boycott their competitions. Are you okay? How do you feel? Is your mom fighting against this . . ."

The words go on and on. I just let them wash over me. Libby's way of caring for someone is to talk. To offer to help. To just go on and on.

I wait for her to talk herself quiet. Finally, there's a little pause.

"Mars?"

"Yeah. I'm here. I—look, Mom got me some ice time at six at Four Corners. Can you come?"

"Of course!"

"That's it. That's all I needed."

After I talk to Libby, I walk to Heather's empty room and thumb through her records.

I finally find what I am looking for. *Aladdin Sane.* Bowie's album with "Panic in Detroit." The cover is striking.

So airbrushed that it's hard to know if it's a painting or a photograph . . . if Bowie is a man or a woman. Or something else. Someone like me.

A red lightning bolt with a blue shadow cuts across the right side of Bowie's face. He's split. Experiencing multiple realities at once. I gently pull the record out from the sleeve and place it on Heather's turntable. Then I place the needle and crank the volume.

Music starts to pour out of the speaker, and I make my way down to the living room, where I can still hear the tune. I don't need to say anything. I don't need to offer an invitation. Mom and Heather are on their feet before the opening riff is done, and then we're all dancing. It's a lot of aggressive jumping up and down. We go on and on and when the last notes ring out, we crash to the floor in a heap.

It's the first time we've done this without Dad here. It takes me a moment to realize that. I didn't even have time to be sad that he isn't here with us. Somehow, doing our ridiculous dance to "Panic in Detroit" brings a part of him into the room with us.

Skating was Dad's and my thing, but now I realize I want to expand the circle. Let others in, so Mom and Heather and I can rekindle Dad.

"Will you come skating with me?" I ask.

▼▲▼

Mom has rented out the rink for just the four—maybe five—of us.

My new black skates are stiff as I lace them up, but they feel good. There's a little room in the toe once they're on my feet. I start doing some squats, bending and forcing the leather to give way to the movement of my ankles.

When the hour starts, I can tell everyone is waiting for me to make the first move. I look at the main door, still hopeful that Jade might walk through. Might still want to be friends.

"Time's ticking, kiddo," Mom says. It's something Dad used to say. I look at her and smile. And then I step out onto the fresh ice. Soon, Libby hops out and whips around the rink. Mom and Heather are less sure on their feet. Mom skates with a kind of delicate slowness, but she bends her knees and seems to move fluidly enough. Heather is a disaster. Skating has never been her thing. I think she went to a few birthday parties at a rink—definitely mine when I was in second and third grades. But now, it's been a few years, and she's stiff. Her knees fight to lock instead of bend to give her support. After I take a lap with Libby, I zip back to Heather and nestle up to her side.

"I'll never know how you got so comfortable on the ice."

"Lots and lots and lots of practice," I say.

"Well, don't spend all of your ice time helping me limp along. That's what the boards are for." I smile and stick with her probably for ten minutes or so. We don't talk, just skate together.

By then Libby has warmed up enough to feel like she can pull out some decent jumps. I skate off and start to join her, beginning with some singles to get the feel for my skates—which are still stiff and sharp. It's not advisable to try my triple this outing, but I'll break them in soon.

After a few jumps, Libby moves to footwork, which I try to follow her on. She's better than me at that, knows all kinds of slick tricks and moves, and I just try to keep up. I cheat, taking an extra step instead of just shifting my edge.

Every so often something catches my eye. Maybe one of the light bulbs is starting to go dead, but the flicker makes me think that someone new is on the ice.

I look up and keep thinking about what it would be like if Jade were here. Stepping on the ice. Maybe she's got her hair in a bun. Maybe it's down, like she had it in that one picture on Instagram. She's late. She didn't have time to get totally ready. So maybe she's wearing jeans with holes so big in the knees you kind of wonder if they are still really pants anymore.

Who cares what she's wearing?

Maybe she's just here.

And maybe that means she doesn't hate me. Maybe she's figured out all of my lies. And if she hasn't yet, maybe she wants to hear me undo them.

Those lies, they grew out of a true place. They grew out of looking for a place in skating. Because after Dad died, skating was the only thing that seemed to stay the same. The

176

jumps. The spins. The way the ice slid beneath my feet. That was the only thing that felt solid when all I could think was, *I miss my dad.* And I'm sad that he's never going to know who I am now and who I'll be.

I look over at Mom, who's pushing through her strokes with a regal precision. I never really skate with her. She's slow, but oddly at ease on her blades. I think about how she kept me on the ice through something really awful. How she hasn't cut her hair since Dad died. And how I worry about that, and I'm not sure why.

And then there's Heather, wobbling her way along the boards and probably counting the seconds until she can remove herself from the ice and retreat to the comfort of solid land. But Heather is stubborn. And hardworking. She thinks that no one sees her, but she managed to land a role in her school musical, so someone must be paying attention. I'm glad. Heather deserves to have people pay attention.

And Libby. Things still feel complicated between us. Having a best friend should be simple, but it isn't. I miss the way things used to be with Libby. And I know that we can't go back. Our friendship has a scar now. A small ugly thing that will always be there, reminding us where we've been.

I hate that she hurt me, but love that she worked to patch us up.

And there's that challenge she made Xander make. That one that started this whole mess . . . but, even though it was confusing, it didn't seem like a mess at first. It seemed like an opportunity to move into a different part of the world I loved.

Because even though I love skating, I had been starting to feel not like me when I had to skate with flourishes and skirts. And so I tried something different. Because that's what you do. When something isn't working, you try something else. And maybe it wasn't the exact right fit, but it was something else. It proves that there are other ways.

I really hope there are ways to skate other than as a girl or a boy. To skate as Mars.

The hour wears on. I fall into making jokes with Libby and exaggerating my style to each of the songs that Heather starts blaring over the sound system—she's abandoned the ice and moved to be sound designer instead. I don't do anything crazy competitive. We just skate around the ice, hooting and hollering, racing from edge to edge every so often. When seven o'clock rolls around, I can't quite believe we've been on the ice for an hour.

Jade doesn't show though. And all of the conversations I imagine having with her stay in my mind.

"The skates seem to work," Mom says as she sits down, rubbing her legs.

"Yeah. Thanks," I say. And, because I realize I haven't said it before, I stand on my blades and walk across the foam floor to throw my arms around Mom.

"It's a lot, kiddo. That's why I'm here. We can handle a lot."

"Yeah."

"Yeah."

The hug goes on for a while. Long enough that I can feel tears starting to stream down my face. I don't want to say goodbye to skating. Maybe skating doesn't want me, but I still want it. And as much as I loved this hour on the ice, I want to break in my black skates fully as I figure out how to do a triple salchow, a triple flip, and a triple lutz—and how to compete with other skaters who are pushing just as hard as I am. Maybe not at Nationals or the Olympics or something, but I want to compete somewhere. Because that's part of the rush.

"I don't want to stop," I say finally.

"You don't have to. We'll figure it out," Mom says with a squeeze.

"Hey, Mars . . ." Libby's voice is kind of quiet, interrupting my moment with my mom with a soft urgency. "She's here."

And there, in the doorway, is Jade. She's not wearing her skating outfit. She's not wearing any of the things I pictured her in.

She's just wearing a pair of sweats and a black T-shirt.

Her hair is in a ponytail, hanging back past her shoulders. And she's got glasses on. I didn't know she wore glasses.

"Jade," I say. My voice is higher than I want. Breathier.

"Hey, Mars." She lifts a tentative hand and gives a wave. "Sorry I didn't make it to skate."

"No, yeah, that's okay," I say.

"I wasn't sure I was gonna come. But . . ." She pauses then. I pin a lot on that word. *But.* She wasn't going to come. *But . . .* here she is.

"Look. I want to be your friend too. Everything is a mess. But I want to be friends."

"Okay." This is so much more than okay. It's stupendous. Miraculous.

"We're gonna head home for some pizza," Mom says. "Do you want to come with us? Libby, you're invited too, of course."

"Are you going to get something other than pineapple on the pizza?" Libby asks.

"Yeah. We obviously are going to get something other than pineapple," Heather scoffs.

"So much for this let's-make-Mars-feel-better party," I say, rolling my eyes dramatically.

"You do feel better. And pineapple is disgusting," says Libby with a laugh.

"Yeah. I can come. I would eat pineapple on pizza," Jade responds.

CHAPTER 20

Pizza is brain food.

By the time the pizza arrives, all of us are sitting in the living room and watching DVRed skating competitions. Normally, I always fast-forward through the human-interest stories between the skates, but I'm not interested in monitoring the remote. During the commercials, we talk about skating and school. Libby tells the story of Xander breaking up with her as a skating partner. Jade tells the story of Xander coming home and declaring that, like Beyoncé, he is better as a solo artist—a line he got from *Schitt's Creek*. The version Jade tells is less dramatic than the fight in the parking lot.

"Just wait until Mars tells you their part."

I pull a pillow into my lap then. Because Mom is here. Heather too. And, well, I haven't told them everything yet.

I know Heather can tell I'm uncomfortable, because she doesn't make a comment like, *Yes, Mars. Please. Do tell*, waggling her eyebrows obnoxiously.

"I like to compete. I like to be challenged. And Xander . . .

he offered that. He's an older skater and good. So I wanted to see how I measured up." I start picking at one of the threads on the pillow. "Honestly, it didn't even really seem like that big of a deal at first, but then as we kept working on it, as Heather got the costume"—Mom gives Heather a look, and Heather shrinks back in her seat a little—"and Libby got recon about Xander's routine . . . it just got bigger and bigger. And I didn't know how to stop it. I didn't even want to try. Because really, when I was on the ice for my turn, it didn't feel like I was doing something wrong. I was just skating. I was just me. And yeah, I ended up being good enough to earn a medal. Them taking my medal isn't the problem. I'm mad that someone really believes I don't belong in a skating competition. Why? Because I don't have a penis? Because I told a lie?" Mom purses her lips a little. "I mean, I get it. Lying is bad. Especially to your mom. But I shouldn't have to lie about this." I beat my hands against my chest when I say the word *this*.

No one talks for a while. They just let my words hang in the air. Maybe they think I'm gonna say more. I don't really have anything else to say.

"You shouldn't have to lie about who you are to compete," Jade says finally. Everyone turns and looks at her. There's something in her tone, in the way she says the words. She's more than just repeating and affirming what I said. She's adding her own idea.

"How long would an open competition run, do you think?" Jade continues. Her eyes are looking off into space, like she's seeing some kind of vision.

"What do you mean by *open*?" I ask.

"Like, the competition is open to anyone who's interested," Jade explains.

I like the sound of that.

But she's continuing on. "Let's say ten people wanted to compete. If you really whizzed through the skaters, how long would that take?"

"Maybe we'd have even more skaters . . . ," Libby chips in, sitting up a little straighter.

"But, like, an hour. Maybe two to be safe?" Jade estimates.

"Yeah, I guess," I say. An open competition? Is that even a thing?

Jade turns to my mom then. "Ms. Hart. You just got Four C for an hour, right? Do you think you could do two?"

"If there was availability. Probably," Mom says.

"Mars, what if we have our own competition? What if me and Libby and you, and whoever else we can get, all skate in an open competition? I'm sure we could find some judges to score us. And we—we just make a space for us to skate."

I look at Jade. Part of what I've always loved about competitions is that they just are. I've never really thought about how they get organized. How they're run.

But when Jade says it, it doesn't sound so hard. Why couldn't we have our own open competition?

I look over at Mom and Heather. Heather smiles; she's already reaching for her computer. Mom just nods. My smile joins theirs . . . Are we going to make this happen?

Jade keeps going. "We get some ice time. We skate. We score. We see how it shakes out. No age brackets. No gender. We just bill it as the best of the best. A chance for people to see how they stack up against anyone else who wants to compete."

Mom pulls out her phone and starts sending a text.

"Who are you texting?" I ask.

"That reporter," she says. "I think we finally have a comment."

Friday at school, Ms. Char is lying in wait.

"Mars. Your paragraph. I know it doesn't seem like a big deal, but the end of the quarter is coming up and I just want to be able to assess where you are."

An assignment for social studies is the last thing on my mind right now. "My paragraph. Right," I say vaguely.

Ms. Char sighs and runs her hand through her hair. "About the unknown person who had a lasting impact on the world."

"Right," I say. I do remember what she's talking about

now. I swear I do. I just . . . don't have time. I've got an open competition to create and run.

"Mars, this really doesn't have to be hard. You could just come in at lunch and write it. Or we could just talk for a little bit about what you want to write about and then you could use dictation to get it on paper."

I nod. I don't really want to give up lunch. It's the one time during the day that I get to see Libby. I haven't braved the eighth-grade lockers since the secret slumber party, but during lunch, Libby always finds me and sits by my side.

But I look at Ms. Char . . . who has been kind and patient, and more than understanding. I don't want to ignore her request.

"Fine," I say.

At lunch, I text Libby to say I will be late, run down to the cafeteria to grab my food, and shuffle back to see Ms. Char.

"Hey, Mars. Thanks for coming."

"I said I would."

"Yes. You did."

Maybe I'm imagining it, but I kind of feel like she's saying, *And you said you would write your paragraph a week ago, but here we are.*

"Who do you want to write on?" Ms. Char asks.

"Honestly, that's been kinda the problem. There are a lot of people who do a lot of things. And I get that they are important and matter and everything, but it's just hard to untangle them."

 185

"Mars, that's a pretty astute observation. A lot of people have spent a lot of time telling us that these conversations aren't connected. That Black Lives Matter has nothing to do with, say, climate change. The thing is, if we don't acknowledge the larger systems at play, what they are rooted in and how they impact everything, we can never hope to make any real progress."

I look at her.

"Sorry, I'm rambling. This is why I became a teacher though." She raises her eyebrows and gives me a little nod, silently asking me to continue, giving me space to talk.

"Okay, well, if the larger system is the one pulling the strings . . . how can someone like me hope to change things? Like, make progress?"

"That's just it. It can be hard to get traction when you start to think about how big the problems are," Ms. Char explains.

I nod. I feel this. I feel this in a big way.

"But it's really important to remember that some action— even a clunky, not quite great action—that's better than nothing."

"Okay."

"Yeah?"

"Yeah. So, uh, I'm working on a project. Can I write about that?"

"Depends. What's the project?"

So I tell her. I tell her how I tried to compete at the Snow Ball, but they stripped me of my award because I wasn't a boy. I tell her about wanting to quit, about throwing my skates into the pond. And then I tell her about Jade's idea for the open competition. My words come out quickly when I get to the part about the competition.

"Wow, Mars. That doesn't seem like a little action. It seems big."

"We're just gonna rent the rink for two hours . . . ," I hedge. But . . . I'm excited. The more I think about the open competition, the more I'm looking forward to it.

"And maybe some other kid, who didn't feel like they could compete because of the system, or who wants to just see a bunch of great skaters, maybe this will open the skating world up to them," Ms. Char says. "Mars, that's huge. And yes, you can write about it. You should write about it. Because other people are going to have things to say about this. And maybe some of them aren't very nice. But you should make sure that you don't lose your voice in all of it."

"Okay."

"I really look forward to reading about it," Ms. Char says.

▼▲▼

I'm nervous. Ms. Char says that the open competition is "huge." Now that it's not just an idea, but a real thing, I'm worried. I keep picturing ways it could fail or fall apart.

Jade and Libby don't share my worry. At school, Libby is talking about the open competition to anyone who will listen, including Rasha. I didn't see Libby throughout the morning, but when I run down for the tail end of lunch after my meeting with Ms. Char, she's still going strong. Talking about how this will be her return to singles skating. How she doesn't have time to build a new routine, so she's going to update her program from last year to add some new skills. How she can't wait to see how she stacks up against everyone.

What she doesn't notice is the way Rasha keeps looking at me while she angrily chews her lunch like a deranged Chihuahua.

At the end of lunch, when we all go to leave, Rasha stops abruptly and turns to me.

"Er, Mars, can we talk for a sec?" she asks, her voice soft. My eyes follow Libby as she and the other eighth graders walk down the hall, oblivious that Rasha has stopped me. I want to shout and call them back. I really don't want to be the victim of middle school girl drama.

But instead, I plant my feet and say, "Sure. What's up, Rasha?"

"Look, you and I, we're not friends."

I nod. Truer words were never spoken.

"But, like, I still want to be friends with Libby," she goes on. Suddenly, she looks a little uncomfortable. "I mean, I get that there is stuff that the two of you share or whatever. Skating . . ."

I nod again. What is this girl getting at?

"And I just want to say, like, can we just not get in each other's way?"

What a strange question. "I dunno," I answer truthfully. "Can we?"

Rasha looks at me like she's lost.

"I mean, it's hard for me to get along with people who call me *it*," I say.

"Right. That."

I wait for her to apologize. To say I misheard her that night at the party. But she doesn't.

"I'll work to not do that again."

"Okay," I say. I don't owe her anything else. I turn to leave, but she puts her hand on my shoulder.

"And you won't take Libby away from me?" she asks.

I turn around and look at Rasha again. While she may have looked lost before, she looks absolutely petrified now. Her eyes are wide, so wide I can see the whites around her brown irises. Her hand is still on my shoulder, and I can feel it shaking ever so slightly.

"Libby makes her own choices," I say. Rasha doesn't relax. There's this little part of me that wants to make Rasha feel comfortable, to help her calm down. I know that Libby wants to be Rasha's friend. That was the crux of our drama. But I just can't bring myself to comfort Rasha. "So, yeah . . ." I really wish I could come up with something more profound to say.

"Okay. Yeah." Rasha repeats my word back to me. Maybe

I would feel bad for her if she hadn't been such a monumental jerk to me for the past year. Maybe we'll get there. But not yet.

After school, Libby comes over to my house. Jade meets us there when her school lets out, and the three of us get to work thinking through the competition before heading out for some ice time.

We start by talking about registration and schedules, mapping out how many competitors can skate in two hours. Jade is a whiz at logistics. I quickly realize that, unlike me, she has thought a lot about how competitions work. It's kind of amazing. Like I needed another reason to think she's totally awesome.

After we discuss logistics, we put Mom and Heather on nailing down our judges—adult skating judges might not take a bunch of teenagers and almost-teenagers seriously.

Then Mom reminds us that our time at Four Corners is coming up, and the three of us tidy the living room and make our way upstairs to change for skating.

We keep talking about the open competition as we change out of jeans and into clothes that will move a little easier on the ice.

"What's tough is that we don't know how many people will show up," Libby points out. "Like, I want it to be more than just the three of us . . ."

I pull my attention away from the conversation to figure out what to wear. My usual skating clothes are in the laundry, so I pull out a pair of leggings and rifle through my drawer to find a shirt that will work.

"We could post about it on Insta . . . ?" Jade offers.

"Oh! A social media push!" Libby sounds excited.

"And, really," Jade continues, "I think Mars should post first." I look up from my shirts to stare at Jade.

"What?" My voice is a squeak. I glance at my phone and think of my own sad Instagram account with my single post and follower. What is posting there gonna do?

"You're the reason for all of this," Jade points out. "Like, Libby and I will share your post, but . . . I dunno . . . I think you should be the one to start."

I'm . . . the reason for all this? Sure, we came up with the idea for the open competition because I didn't have anywhere else to compete. But I think about how Libby has been babbling all day about it and how it has given her a way to get back into singles skating. I think about how Jade is so incredible at understanding how competitions work, and this project is giving her a chance to really dig into that interest. Then I think about . . . someone I don't know. Someone who might also need this competition and doesn't know it yet.

"Okay . . . ," I say. "I'll take a picture in my skates at Four C and then post."

"I didn't even know you had an Instagram," Libby says.

"They're @SkatingOn*Mars*, with stars around 'Mars,'" Jade says offhandedly.

Libby gives me a look. I immediately blush, which makes

Libby almost bust out laughing. For a quick moment, I'm scared she's going to say something embarrassing about how obvious my crush on Jade is, but she doesn't. She really is a good friend.

"Come on, just pick a shirt so we can go!" Libby finally says.

I pull out an oversized shirt from the bottom of my drawer. It's pink with Bowie's lightning bolt splashed across the front. I forgot I even had this shirt. Even though I'm not much of a pink person, I pull it on over my head. The fabric is soft and worn. Yeah, I can skate in this.

When our hour on the rink starts, I step out and snap a picture of the toes of my black skates against the milky white of the ice. I opt not to use a filter, and quickly type:

These are my new black skates. I'm excited to try them out against anyone who wants to compete on Sunday. No age divisions. No gender divisions. Let's just skate and see what happens. Details in bio.

I click share and notice that **@LibSTAR~*** has followed me. I follow Libby back and give her and Jade a thumbs-up. The two of them pull out their phones and start typing up their own posts. I turn my attention to the ice and begin warming up, working my way up to my triple and then shifting to my step sequence and those pesky twizzles.

We aren't the only people on the ice tonight, but everyone seems pretty focused on their own work. I'm startled when about halfway through the hour, Jade comes up and taps me on the shoulder.

"Think about attacking it the way you attack a jump," she says. Her voice is a little breathless.

"What?" I say.

"I've seen you work on jumps. Twizzles really aren't that different. Just . . . less exciting, I guess. But you need the same confidence and the same persistence."

I nod. Jumps have always been my strong suit. And maybe that's partly for the reason Jade thinks. But there is also something so clear about jumps. The height, the number of rotations . . . you either land, or you fall. Footwork is harder . . . not because it isn't technical, but because you have to look close to suss out what's happening.

"Earth to Mars!" Jade says. She wrinkles her nose and laughs a little at her own joke.

"Sorry . . . you . . . you're right. I haven't been thinking about footwork and jumps in the same way."

"Might be worth a try," Jade says with a shrug. Then she's off, winding up for a double axel. She lands it clean—no under-rotation. She's been working.

I run through my program a few times without music, just imagining the tune in my head. I'm able to get through it, but something feels off. I look at Libby and Jade, who are both practicing new elements that they plan to add to their programs for the open competition.

I hadn't been planning on changing anything. But then I catch my reflection in the plastic that lines the rink, the David Bowie lightning bolt streaking down my chest. And it comes to me. I know exactly what I'm going to change: my music. I spend the rest of the practice running the routine, hearing the new song in my head. I'm winded by the time our hour wraps up, and I wish I weren't so sweaty when Jade gives me a quick hug before hopping into her dad's car.

Libby raises her eyebrows at me after Jade leaves, and I tell her to shut her face. Libby cackles as she climbs into her ride. Then it's just me . . . and without the excited chatter of Jade and Libby, I start to worry.

"What if no one comes?" I say to Mom as I get in the van. "What if it's just me?"

"And Jade," Mom adds. "And Libby."

"Yeah. Just the three of us. Isn't that . . . kind of pathetic?" I look down at my knees.

"So what if no one comes? You still get to skate. You still get to be scored. You can just work for a personal best."

Suddenly, a message comes through my phone in my group text with Jade and Libby. It's a link from Libby to Jade's Instagram.

I open the link, and there's a picture of me. It's from the Snow Ball. The one that ran in the article.

The caption reads:

Hey everyone. This is Mars. They are a friend of mine. Last weekend, Mars skated in the Snow Ball. You may remember seeing them. Maybe you don't. If you missed it, it was a great skate. What happened afterward wasn't so great. Because Mars isn't a boy, the MFSA took away their silver medal. Maybe you agree with that decision. But if you're anything like me, you don't. You think that was wrong. So . . . if you want to support Mars . . . if you want to skate against them, if you just want to see some of the best skating on the planet, maybe come to the first ever open competition at Four Corners. Details in bio.

Just as I finish reading the caption, but before I tumble into absolute and utter delight about Jade publicly supporting me, another message from Libby comes in: **Check out the comments!**

I flip back to the post and scroll down to read through the comments.

> **I'm in.**
> **Can't wait.**
> **Wouldn't miss it.**

There's a sea of affirmations. In about an hour. We have . . . other people.

But one comment in particular has accrued a lot of interest.

@{Uni}TYonIce: I got to skate against Mars, and they made me push to up my game. You better believe I'm coming back for more on Sunday!

Under the comment are about a dozen replies saying that they can't wait to see the matchup. That they're in even though they know they'll be throttled. That they're excited to be a part of the competition.

> Libby: Did you see?! Ty Cobalt! He's gonna come to our competition!
> Me: Wow! Thx Jade!
> Jade: You started it!

I blush a little. My heart hammers as I text back.

> Me: Yeah
> Me: But I only have TWO followers

I'm downplaying my post a little, but I'm proud. And still amazed that this is actually going to happen.

> Jade: Just takes the RIGHT two followers

I screenshot the text exchange right away and fleetingly think about printing it out and framing it. Jade's really got a way with emojis.

On Saturday, the three of us decide to have a dress rehearsal. Heather drives me to practice, and when I'm about to get out of the car, she hands me a bag.

"We have to replace that pirate shirt. It looks ridiculous."

I open the bag. Inside there's a pair of thick black leggings with some quilting on the knees down to the shins. There's also a shirt. It's a little flowy with short sleeves—shorter than a T-shirt. I unfold it, and splashed across the front is a sequined red-and-blue lightning bolt, just like the cover of *Aladdin Sane*. In the bottom of the bag there's a jar of some kind of hair product called Glitter Hair Cement.

It's perfect.

Particularly since I've decided to change my music at the last minute.

"Bring some panic to the skate," Heather says. "I'm getting a coffee."

When I walk in, Jade is waiting in her purple skating outfit, and Libby's got a frothy pink feathered confection on.

I smile when I see them. My friends. Our friendships haven't always been steady, but they're still standing.

"Is that what you're wearing?" Libby asks, looking at my sweats.

I roll my eyes. "No, Heather just gave me my skating costume. I'll go get dressed."

When I get to the bathrooms, I'm not sure where to go,

but I'm surprised to see that the sign on the accessible bathroom has changed. No longer is it just the normal wheelchair. It also has a classic-looking bathroom stick figure that is half man, half woman. Next to the new sign there's a note: WE WELCOME ANYONE AT OUR RINK. YOU CAN USE ANY RESTROOM THAT MAKES YOU FEEL COMFORTABLE.

I blink. It hadn't occurred to me that *anyone* was paying attention to what made me comfortable. Not really. I reach and go into the single-stall bathroom and change quickly. I open the Glitter Hair Cement, glop some of it on my hair, and push the strands so they're standing up wildly at every angle.

When I come out of the bathroom, Libby whistles. "Oh, Mars. That's just not fair!"

I notice Jade tug on the skirt of her dress self-consciously.

"C'mon. Let's skate," I say.

CHAPTER 21

After Jade's post blew up, I started following everyone who said something nice about the tournament or said they were planning to compete. A few followed me back. But not many. Why would they? I still only just have my photos of the van dashboard captioned **It's a Bowie kind of day** and the tips of my black skates announcing the open competition.

I keep checking my phone throughout the night, wanting to see if anyone else who needs our competition has found it. Maybe I'm also trying to keep from absolutely freaking out.

When I feel my eyelids insisting on closing, I walk over to my dresser and pull on Dad's Michigan sweatshirt. There's this part of me that feels like I should make some declaration, whisper about how tomorrow is all about him. But . . . it isn't. Sure, a part of it is. A part of everything that I do is about Dad in some way. But this competition. This skate. It's for me.

When I wake up on Sunday, the sun isn't even up, but Mom is already at the kitchen table. "You feeling ready for today?"

"I don't know. I mean, I'm just happy that I get to skate." The last word is punctuated by a yawn.

"I know. But it's okay if it's more complicated than that."

I nod. Then I take a breath. "Do you wanna walk to the pond with me?" I ask. I'm not sure why, but I just . . . I want to go there. And I want Mom to come. Even though she never has before.

"If you want," she says. "I assume that's all you're willing to wear." She gestures at Dad's sweatshirt. "Like father, like da— child." She corrects herself midword. I run up and hug her. She threads her arms under mine and squeezes me back. It's not a courtesy squeeze either. This is a full-blown mega-hug. We're both clinging to each other, just soaking in the way it feels to be totally surrounded by someone who loves you.

When we finally disentangle, I slide my hand into Mom's, and we make our way out the door. We don't talk as we walk to the woods at the edge of the neighborhood. Our breath is misty, forming small clouds in the cold air against the dim glow of early morning.

Mom doesn't say anything when we get to the pond. Maybe she's waiting for me to break the silence.

"I wish Dad were here," I say finally.

"Me too," she says softly. "For so many reasons."

"It's hard . . . turning into someone new without him." What I don't say is that I feel guilty. I feel like all of the things that have happened over the past weeks have changed me. And moved me away from Dad. From the person Dad knew.

"You're still you."

"But I'm not Veronica," I say. "Are you sad I'm not her? Do you think he would be?"

"Mars." Mom says my name a little louder. "You have always been you. You will always be you. I'm so glad that you've found a way to be a version of you that feels more . . . you-like." She takes a deep breath. "I'm not going to pretend I know what your dad would say . . . Maybe he'd crack a joke or spend hours figuring out which Bowie song is your new personal anthem. Maybe he would mess up your name and your pronouns. But he would figure it out. Because he loves you. And he would be proud. Because he was proud of you. Always."

I smile, thinking about this version of life where Dad knows me now. I live in that world for a minute, imagining that when Mom and I get back from the pond, Dad will be in the kitchen making chocolate chip pancakes in the shape of Mickey Mouse and jokingly complaining that he wasn't invited to the pond.

But when we get home, he isn't there.

I go through the morning routine. Breakfast, shower, stretch, and dress. I snap a picture of myself in the mirror and open Instagram. It's full of similar pictures. Skaters sizing themselves up before competition. I hit the plus sign and post my first selfie.

We make our way to Four Corners at about nine o'clock to set things up. After offering a heartfelt apology to me and

Mom a few days ago, Martha and Deb offered to run the registration table at the open competition. Heather is going to be working in the sound booth—announcing skaters and playing the music. Mom managed to secure five judges.

Any worry I have about no one showing up disappears immediately when we arrive at Four Corners. The parking lot is fuller than normal on a Sunday, and when I walk in, a few people say, "Hey, Mars!" as I hunt down a spot to keep my bag. It's weird. Off the ice, I always wanted to be invisible. I've never felt like people see me when I'm not skating. Let alone know who I am. But as people greet me, I realize that it's nice to be known.

"Mars!" a deep voice rings out. I look up, and there's Ty.

"Hey!" I say, throwing a hand up, matching the way he spreads all of his fingers apart. "Thanks for coming . . ."

"Elena Bolinkhov is here today. That's wild. She's bound for Nationals this year, and she's *here*, and I get to see how I stack up."

"What?" I'm not computing.

"Did you know? People from all over the Midwest are coming in to compete. Everyone's curious to see how they measure up. Plus, it's not always a given that we get an attentive audience. I think a lot of people are excited to see how this goes. Anyway, see you out there."

The crowd is unbelievable. The bleachers are packed with babbling spectators. Part of me wishes I could be up there, watching these skaters from all over come together and compete. It's the first time I wish that my pre-skate routine didn't take me away from other skaters, because meeting everyone is fun. But the moments before my skate have always been about making everything else go away, not about seeing who else is out there. As I hunt down an empty hallway to stretch and run through my routine, I open Instagram and scan through. My feed is filled with dozens of selfies at 4C. It's incredible.

There's a DM from Jade waiting for me.

@Jade$k8s: Good luck.

@SkatingOn*Mars*: You too.

My eyes are still glued to my phone when I run into another skater. A tall, muscular figure. I look up, and there, standing in front of me, is Xander.

"Hey, watch where you're—" he starts, before he even knows it's me. When he finally registers my face, he freezes. "Oh, it's you."

My whole body is tense. I'm in a back hallway with the person who is responsible for making my life over the past week absolute trash.

What is he doing here at all?

"You're probably wondering why I'm here."

I don't say anything.

"I want to beat you. For real. Not because of a technicality."

"You have the rest of skating. Can't I just have my corner?"

"I thought this was open to anyone," Xander says.

"It is," I finally respond.

"Well, I'm anyone."

"You certainly are."

"So, what do you say?" he asks. Challenging me the way he always does.

"I . . ." Just then Jade comes around the corner, no doubt looking for a spot of her own. She freezes when she sees me and Xander.

"Hey, Juju," Xander says, smiling and cocking an eyebrow.

I feel a little hurt then. Because Jade and I spent so much time together . . . And here's her brother, ruining everything. And she didn't tell me he was coming!

"What are you doing here, Xander?" she asks. Okay, maybe she didn't lie. Maybe she just didn't know.

"Look, I listened to what you said, Jade. About how I was being narrow-minded and . . . well, I'm . . . I'm here. I'm gonna compete."

"I didn't say it to make you compete. I said it to make you see that you had done something hurtful and wrong."

"Can't it be both?"

Jade rolls her eyes and comes to stand next to me. She pushes her hand into mine, brushing her long fingers against my ragged ones.

I stand a little taller and say, "You wanna know what I say, Xander? I say you owe me an apology. And then, if you are

204

able to do that? Bring it on." The words sound so confident coming out of my mouth.

Xander runs his hand over the back of his neck and looks around the hallway like he wants to leave. Jade squeezes my hand a little, and I feel my heart start to sputter.

"Yeah. Okay. Sorry."

I wait a little bit. Wondering if that's it. Wondering why I don't feel better.

"Okay. Well, I look forward to beating you again," I say, letting overconfidence color my words. "Now, can you let me practice?"

Xander just rolls his eyes and stalks off, his large bag slamming against his back.

"Well, that was something," Jade finally says.

"Yeah. A small, clumsy step is better than nothing."

I'm in the first flight, skating second out of thirty-three skaters total. Normally, I hate going early in a comp. I like knowing where the bar is when it's my turn to skate.

But today? Today, I'm okay with second.

So I lace up my black skates a little before eleven and take the ice for warm-ups. Those first moments on the ice almost feel normal. Eight or nine of us are skating at a time, and everyone is out quick, working hard to scuff up every bit of the ice. I try not to look at the other jumps, the other spins. I

try not to be intimidated. I focus on my own legs, on bending them and feeling the way my skates still creak against the
pressure. I do a few low jumps and then start gaining speed.
I hit my triple. I hit it again. Three times, and I'm out. I've
got it. It's going to happen. The buzzer sounds, and everyone makes their way off the ice. Libby is also skating in the
first flight and makes a point of coming over and bumping
my hip.

"Pretty cool, huh?"

"Yeah."

I don't pay attention to what the first skater does. What
jumps they land, what spins they nail. I'm sitting with my
earbuds in, just thinking through my routine as I listen to
my music one last time. I dwell on the few new tricks I've
added. The twizzles that Jade forced me to learn. The extra
toe loop at the end of the double salchow.

I'm up sooner than I'd like. As soon as I step out, before
I can do anything, the crowd lets out a roar. It's unlike anything I've heard before. I'm not sure what people are screaming, but when I look out, I can see that most of them are up
on their feet.

Heather's voice comes over the speaker. "Now skating:
Mars Hart."

The screams get even louder then. I can't even really think;
there's only cheers.

I skate a quick lap and move to the center of the ice. When
I give Heather a nod, the crowd gets quiet. It's incredible. I

push the air out of my lungs, and when the music pipes in, I breathe in through my nose and take off.

I've picked new music for this competition. "Panic in Detroit."

Two weeks ago, skating was about forgetting that I lost Dad. Forgetting that I was a confused enby kid. But that's not what it is now. Now it's about embracing all of those pieces of me and maybe even sharing them.

After my flip, there are a few claps, but when I land the triple and throw a double toe loop on the end, the spectators are on their feet again. The rest of the program is a blur. Skating is so often just about me, ice, and gravity; but today, today it's about me, ice, gravity . . . and the world seeing us together. I'm smiling—something I don't normally do in competition—as I move through the complicated footwork pass that Jade added to my program, fly through my double flip, and launch into my final layback spin (the one that Libby helped me master).

When the whole thing ends, I pump my fist in the air and dip my head. I try to hold it together for three seconds before I slip out of my final pose and let the cheers wash over me as I fall to my knees.

I press my face into my hands, overwhelmed by the skate, the crowd, the whole thing.

I'm not sure how long the cheers go on. Maybe two seconds, maybe two full minutes, but suddenly there's a tap on my shoulder. It's Jade, who has run out onto the ice in her sneakers. She reaches a hand toward me, and I take it. She tugs hard, pulling me into a hug. I'm not sure I've ever experienced a better hug in my life. The crowd roars again, and I can feel my cheeks getting red and blotchy. Not that I care.

"We did it," Jade whispers.

Suddenly, there's another pair of arms. Libby's there too. Babbling about how she can't believe she has to follow that. I bump her with my hip and turn to the crowd and give them a wave. Then I offer up Libby with a flourish of my arms.

Heather's voice comes over the speaker system again. "Now skating: Libby Groh-Stearn."

The rest of the competition passes in a blur. Not an angry blur or a slow blur. It's a happy blur. A blur that I never want to end. After I take off my skates, I pull on a fleece and snuggle in on the bleachers with Mom to watch the rest of the competition.

But I'm not watching it like a competition. I'm watching everyone the way Jade does. She said she just wants people to see the skill and art of the sport instead of getting hung up on the scores.

Ty's routine is flawless even though he's added an element since the Snow Ball. Xander delivers a clean performance and has been working on his triple. I'm going to have to keep working if I want to keep up. But there's more. Elena, the skating phenomenon who's bound for Nationals, planned three triples and executes two of them in competition. Mark, who's only ten, knocks everyone out with his speed and gusto. Jade's got the crowd in the palm of her hand by about second five.

In the end, I'm not even sure I care how the scoring ends up.

Okay. I'm lying. I definitely care about the scores.

When they're finally tabulated, Heather announces over the loudspeaker that a skater named Sam claims bronze, Ty captures silver, and Elena earns gold.

I keep waiting for my name to come out. For her to say, *And also there is a double first place, and that's Mars.* But it doesn't come. Just bronze, silver, and gold. The crowd is a little hectic as everyone goes out. A few people ask me to take selfies with them. One person has a Polaroid camera and asks me to sign the photo once it develops.

The hallway where the final scores are posted is crowded, and it's hard to know if I will ever be able to get close enough to see how I did.

It isn't until about a half hour later that the crowd thins enough for me to get up to the score sheet.

I look at it, and there I am. Sixth. My scores are solid, higher than at the Snow Ball, but other people here are just better. The field is stronger.

I take a picture of the sheet with my phone and walk back toward the main lobby area. Mom's there, and her eyebrows are furrowed.

"You okay?" she asks.

"Yeah. I got sixth," I say. I try to sound, I dunno . . . chipper? But I'm not. I wanted to win. Or at least get on the podium.

"I saw," Mom says.

"Better than my first competition," I say, trying to crack a joke. It doesn't work.

Just then, Jade comes running up. I feel a sharp pang of guilt as I realize that I didn't even check her scores. Or Libby's. I mean, I know they weren't in the top six. I only cared about how I placed.

"Mars! This was amazing! We did it! We thought what? A handful of people would show up? Look what we did! All these people, they all . . . they all *want* to be here. They *want* to do this." I've never heard Jade babble before.

Libby's there too. "That was seriously the best competition I've ever participated in. I mean, come on! It was stacked! Like . . . totally wild."

I nod, thinking about the triple axel Ty pulled out and Elena's flawless Biellmann spin, where she twirled clutching the blade of her skate over her head.

Jade and Libby are right. This competition *was* amazing. And . . . with that field, I still pulled out a sixth-place finish. I didn't win, but I proved that I've got a place on the ice. And who knows what will happen next time, after I am able to refine my footwork, make my jumps combinations, and add more triples?

My mind is racing about what I need to do next to make my program more competitive, and about how I need to find a new skating coach, as Jade and Libby gush about the competition and finally decide that we should all head to Dairy Queen for celebratory Blizzards.

When I get into the van with Mom, she says, "Dmitri and Katya came. I invited them. I didn't want to tell you. But if you still want to work with them, they said that they were wrong. That your talent is impressive no matter your gender and that they are excited to keep working with you. I told them we would talk about it. And that it's your choice."

Oh. Wow. I was . . . not expecting that. "Okay. Do I have to pick now?"

"No. You can go at whatever pace you want."

"I just don't know if . . . I don't know if Katya and Dmitri are the right fit for me right now. Or if . . . if I need something else." There's a lot to think about. But it's kind of great to imagine that I have a future on the ice. As me. Mars.

"Okay. Well, we'll figure out the next steps. But first, let's celebrate this last step. Dairy Queen?"

"Yeah, definitely."

▼▲▼

Mars Hart
4 November (Late! Sorry)
I never really thought of myself as an activist. And I never thought I would make a lasting impact on the world. All I ever wanted to do was skate.

I learned to skate when I was four. Long before I knew I was nonbinary. Long before my dad died. Long before I had any clue what the MFSA was. But skating saw me through all of those challenges.

For a long time, I couldn't figure out if I was a boy or a girl. It wasn't until I heard the word *nonbinary* that I really started to understand my gender. Even though parts of my physical body sometimes felt strange to me, skating always felt good. I'm at home in my body when I skate.

When my dad died, skating was the only thing that made me feel better. Skating was a reason to get up in the morning. The ice rink was a place that still made sense when the rest of the world didn't.

And then came another challenge. The MFSA. Michigan Figure Skating Association. That's when skating almost went away for me. As a nonbinary skater, I don't fit into a preset competition category. I thought that I could just pretend I was a boy or a girl in order to compete, but when I was told I couldn't compete as a part of the MFSA men's competition, I learned that skating is a part of a larger system, one that insists on binaries to organize everything.

That system is at odds with who I am. I'm not a man or a woman, so those categories don't really work for me. So I had to make a choice. Give up a part of myself or give up competitive skating.

I chose to make a third option. I decided to make my own rules. My own tournament. An open tournament, available to anyone who wanted to compete.

I'm not sure where things will go next. If there will be other tournaments I can compete in or if the rules and regulations will change . . . but I hope that someone saw the open competition and realized that the world doesn't have to stay the same. I now know that it's worth trying to make space for everyone in the world. That's the impact I hope I am able to make.

ACKNOWLEDGMENTS

I'll start by thanking you. Either you've gotten to the end of Mars's story and are still reading, or you skipped straight to the acknowledgments (I do that too). Whatever your reasons, thank you for being here. Thank you for supporting this book and allowing this story into your life.

One person is particularly responsible for my continued work as a writer over the past six years: Jamie Rubenstein. Jamie believed in my words when I didn't and gave me a space to process the ups and downs of being an author.

This story wouldn't be in your hands if it weren't for my agent, Jessica Mileo, at InkWell Management, who lost power one Friday in December 2020 and fortunately had an early draft of *Skating on Mars* downloaded. Jess saw Mars and loved all parts of them—from their competitive streak to their soft heart. The publishing world is a lot less intimidating with Jess and the InkWell team in my corner.

The idea of someone picking apart your words is a little terrifying . . . or it would be if it weren't for my editor, Rachel Diebel. Rachel's belief in this book was always palpable—in every call and email. Every note, question, and suggestion was rooted in making the story better. *Skating on Mars* is clearer and stronger for her exceptional work.

I'd also like to thank the wonderful team at Feiwel and Friends—Jean Feiwel, L. Whitt, Helen Seachrist, and Kim Waymer, in particular. Additional thanks to Jackie Dever for her sharp eye and kind comments when it came time for copy edits, and Violet Tobacco for her incredible cover illustration. It takes so many people to make a book!

Thanks to Dad, Mari, Greg, Maggie, Pete, and John, who have been there for (really) bad times and celebrated the good ones. Thanks to Kelly, Monica, Peggy, and Quincy, who always remind me to take care of myself. Thanks to Jen, Justine, Kate, Ronnie, and Edward, who provide boundless enthusiasm and support. Thanks to my students, who prove that adapting to the new is never as hard as people sometimes make it out to be.

I didn't know I was a writer until I was thirty-three. I didn't know I was nonbinary until I was thirty-five. I have no doubt there is much about myself that I will learn in the coming years. Maybe you already have an idea of who you are. Maybe you're on your way. Or maybe you haven't started yet. Wherever and whoever you are: I'm glad you're here.

Thank you for reading this Feiwel & Friends book. The friends
who made **SKATING ON MARS** possible are:

Jean Feiwel, Publisher
Liz Szabla, VP, Associate Publisher
Rich Deas, Senior Creative Director
Holly West, Senior Editor
Anna Roberto, Senior Editor
Kat Brzozowski, Senior Editor
Dawn Ryan, Executive Managing Editor
Kim Waymer, Senior Production Manager
Emily Settle, Editor
Rachel Diebel, Editor
Foyinsi Adegbonmire, Associate Editor
Brittany Groves, Assistant Editor
L. Whitt, Designer
Helen Seachrist, Senior Production Editor

Follow us on Facebook or visit us online at mackids.com.
Our books are friends for life.